Dog Gone and Dead

Book 5 in
The New Orleans Go Cup Chronicles series

By Colleen Mooney

DOG GONE and DEAD is Book 5 in The New Orleans Go Cup Chronicles series
Copyright © 2018, Colleen Mooney all Editions
Print Edition

Paperback ISBN 978-0-9905527-9-6

Prologue

THIS WAS WAY too early on a Saturday morning for any dog to go outside. It was still dark; the woman was half awake, so she didn't realize the leash didn't connect to his collar. She blamed herself for not hooking him to the leash before she picked him up and carried him across the highway to the beach side. She tried calling him a couple of times before she realized he was not paying attention and already had a good lead on her. The wind was blowing in her face so it was unlikely he could even hear her.

After wrapping the leash around her wrist like a bracelet, she took off running after him as fast as she could. *That Rascal,* she thought, *he lives up to his name.* As soon as she stood up thinking he was hooked to his leash, he broke free and headed toward the water. The sand was deep where the woman stood. Rascal was making more progress. Rascal had the advantage of four-paw drive, and he was running closer to the water's edge where there was firmer footing. She made her way over to the wet sand.

In the darkness Rascal was barely visible and the

distance between them was expanding. The full moon reflected off the sand giving just enough light to spot him up ahead. He was having a gay ole time running as fast as he could. She'd never catch him if he kept up this pace. When she got closer to the pier she was afraid she would lose him for good. He would be out of sight for a few seconds. He might turn left and make his way to the parking lot and over to one of the neighborhoods across the highway.

Running along the wet packed sand made it easier to control her breathing and she picked up her pace thankful for a routine of morning runs. It was good training for chasing this guy along the beach. She wished he would stop and sniff something, and then she could catch up to him.

When she got to the pier, she didn't slow her pace. When she ran under it, something hit her hard on the back of the head. As she fell, stunned, she thought something tripped her. It was harder to see in the shadows under the pier. When she turned to see what it could be, someone stepped out from the darkness. Her last thought was *what would happen to her sister and little Rascal now if this guy got his hands on them.*

Chapter One

SUNRISE BROKE THE darkness in Jiff's family condo overlooking the Gulf of Mexico waking me up with its arrival. My boyfriend, Jiff Heinkel, and I both live in New Orleans. We were finally on a much-needed weekend alone. Even in late February, the weather was perfect, not too hot and not too cool. My name is Brandy Alexander, and I love the beach this time of year. We might get a cool snap, but it's normally very nice weather with no one around to share the beach with.

His condo was the penthouse, seventeen stories up on Gulf Boulevard, with a spectacular view of the Florida beach with its pure white sand and turquoise blue water. I couldn't wait to go for a swim. We had gone to bed leaving the sliding door open to listen to the soft sound of waves rushing onto the beach. It worked its magic as the sound carried up to our room with the sea air and lulled us to sleep.

While this was a family stretch of waterfront con-dos I always loved to come in the late winter or early spring before the families and college kids littered the sand. I find the beach is better enjoyed without music blasting. I could do without dodging volleyballs or footballs, tripping over water rafts, sand toys, and hearing the playful screaming that came along on family vacations.

I nudged Jiff and whispered in his ear, "C'mon, let's go for a walk before anyone else is up."

"No one else is up," he said, rolled over and put a pillow over his head. I heard a muffled, "What time is it?"

"Almost six-thirty," I said and pulled the pillow off his face so I could try to kiss him awake. It was really only six-o-five.

"We're on vacation. The beach will still be deserted at nine. No one goes out before noon," he grumbled and with his eyes still closed reached around for his pillow.

"I'll go by myself," I said, bouncing off the bed.

"Okay, just give me a sec," he said, but he laid there a few more minutes.

"I already have my suit on," I called from the bathroom. I combed my shoulder length, blonde hair and pulled it up in a ponytail. I stepped into a black, one-piece bathing suit that only covered what a bikini should cover and the rest of the suit had mesh holding it together. I took a second to admire the hours I had put in at the gym all winter and I was pleased with the results. I added a black and white cloth hat that had a floppy look about it. It could roll up and be stuck under a shoulder strap if I got tired of wearing it.

"Here," I said throwing his swim trunks on the bed. "You don't even need to get up to get dressed. C'mon. It's beautiful out there right now. Just you, me and the beach."

When we made it to the sand, Jiff was still walking like a Zombie. Going through the loose, deep sand I thought he looked a little tipsy since he wasn't fully awake until I realized he had his eyes shut.

"Even with my eyes closed, I can tell we are on the beach," he said. "I feel sand between my toes." He removed his sunglasses and rubbed his eyes for the umpteenth time.

"I thought you might be sleep walking because you haven't said anything about my new suit. I bought it just for this trip," I said. "You know I love the beach."

Jiff made an effort to open both eyes wide. He looked me up and down taking in my new bathing suit and said, "I know you love the beach. And I love you."

Wait. What? This was the first time he said I love you. It felt as though something sucked the air off the entire beach. I didn't want to make too much out of it or too little. I casually added, "I love you, too."

He scooped me up off my feet and spun around. He was fully awake now. When he set my feet back in the sand he said, "I'll race you to the pier," and took off running.

"Oh, you've been playing me, you big cheater!" I yelled at his back.

I was never going to catch him since he had too much of a lead and a much longer stride. He also had run track in high school and college while I had run my mouth. I saw him ahead of me. He stopped sharply and turned away from the water's edge under the pier. He stood looking down at something. Something that looked like a beach towel or blanket all balled up.

When I approached, Jiff turned and said, "No, don't come closer. This is bad."

"What? What is it?" Leaning around him I managed to get a look at the top part of the girl that was on the sand and half floating in the water. "Oh, no. That poor girl. Did she drown?"

"I'm not sure, but from the look of her, I don't think she's been in the water. I see bruising around her neck. We need to call the police," Jiff said looking up and down the beach to see if there was anyone else around.

"We left our cell phones in the room."

"Yeah. Look, walk back away in your own footprints in the sand so we don't contaminate this crime scene any more than we already have," Jiff said. He was an attorney in his dad's criminal law practice and had defended a friend of mine in the past.

"I'll stay here and make sure no one else walks up on her," I said trying to see what was wrapped around her wrist.

"No, I'll stay here and you run up to the street and see if you can find a phone or someone with a phone. I don't want you alone if someone is still lurking about," Jiff said.

"Okay," I said and squatted down to get a better look at what was wrapped around her wrist. It was a dog's leash wound partially around the woman's arm with the end floating in the water lapping at her side. "Look, she must have been walking her dog, but where's the dog?" I could feel Jiff getting ready to react to my being so close to the woman. I held up my hand and added, "I'm not going to touch anything."

"I don't want to move her. The local police will love that but she might be floating away soon and the water might destroy evidence," he said.

Before I stood up, I looked up and down the beach and said, "I think it's safe to say she lost Rascal and Rascal is a Schnauzer."

"Rascal? How do you know he's a Schnauzer?" he asked looking up and down the beach mimicking me.

Schnauzers were our thing. Well, it was definitely my thing. I rescued them and found homes for those people had abandoned or left at shelters. I had one and Jiff had one. He saw me bringing a rescue to a man in his condo complex and shortly after that we had a chance meeting and started dating. It sounds simple, but like Tina Turner… I never do anything nice and easy, not even when it came to meeting the man of my dreams.

I pointed to the part of the leash that had unwound from her wrist. It showed an image of a little salt and pepper schnauzer stitched right in front of RASC. "I'm guessing that's the first part of the dog's name on this leash," I said. "It's one your special-order sets with the dog's name and a picture of the breed on it. Sometimes the collar has the owner's phone number stitched into it like the name is on the leash." I started to point closely to one section on the woman's wrist. "Look right here…"

"Don't touch it." Jiff said it so loud I jumped. "Sorry."

"Give me some credit, please." I had picked us a small thin piece of driftwood. Using it I lifted the part of the fabric floating in the water so he could see the part I could see still on her wrist. "There's a Schnauzer image stitched right next to the name. I'm guessing the name is Rascal. I was going to order my Meaux and your Isabella one for next Christmas."

I carefully walked in my own footsteps back up the beach while Jiff took a couple of steps back and yelled, "I'll wait here and keep anyone else from walking up on her, but don't let anyone see you in that swim suit."

I looked at him, shook my head, shrugged my shoulders up asking him, "So do you think I should take it off to go look for a phone?"

"I wish I had put on a T-shirt," he said.

Chapter Two

T HE ONLY PLACE I found open at six-twenty-five a.m., was a Tom Thumb Gas Station and Convenience Store across the street from the fishing pier. I felt exposed with no beach cover-up over my suit but it did get the attention of the clerk behind the counter. He let me use the phone to call the police. I'm not even sure he heard me say I found a dead woman under the pier.

By the time I got back to Jiff, two uniformed police officers were already there marking off the area with crime scene tape. A barefoot guy, with BEACH PATROL written in large yellow lettering across the back of his very tight, black, neoprene shirt, was helping them.

Jiff was standing back away from the area where they were working near the dune buggy I assumed the Beach Patrol dude arrived on.

"Did you ask Surfer Boy over there," I said nodding to the shaggy haired guy wearing the beach patrol billboard, "if he saw a Schnauzer running loose?"

"No. I didn't. I think Surfer Boy is some sort of auxiliary cop. I think that's a gun under those beach jams. He came screaming up on that thing so I'm sure he thought I was his prime suspect. I told him what we found, and that you went to call the police leaving me to keep anyone from disturbing the crime scene. He called it in on his radio. The two uniforms were here in under a minute." Jiff said.

"I was probably still looking for a phone. This is a little different from trying to help the police in New Orleans, huh?" I asked him when we were downwind from the three of them.

"Yes, the two in uniform thanked me and said they were grateful I stayed to keep anyone from touching the body after we found it," he said. "They are very efficient, and polite. Surfer Boy seems a little full of himself."

"Even growing up next door to Dante didn't get me polite, let alone preferential, treatment. Since the holidays, I'm not sure there isn't some trumped up warrant out for my arrest," I said trying to be funny, but Jiff looked serious.

"Now that you mention it, I'll check to see if he has any outstanding warrants filed on you when we get back," he said and kissed my forehead.

My once, almost fiancé is now Captain Dante Deedler in the New Orleans Police Department. We have been permanently estranged since Christmas Eve. This is all due to the covert efforts of family members meddling in my life. Even our family housekeeper plotted against me. They all conspired and got me to his home on Christmas Eve so he could propose in front of everyone. This is after I had not seen or heard from Dante in weeks. It wasn't because he was in Iraq or somewhere fighting a war. No-o-o-o-o-o, he was downtown, about four miles away, working every day until he left for Houston for a three-day conference right before Christmas.

When he finally called from the conference a day before Christmas Eve—he told me it would be a good idea if I made other plans for the holidays. He didn't think he'd get a flight back to New Orleans for a few more days. The call was brief. He hung up on me before I could tell him I had been making other plans without him since—before Thanksgiving—the last time I had not heard from him.

Woozie, my parent's housekeeper, tricked me when she showed up unannounced at my apartment and asked for a ride to my parents' house. When I got there I had been mortified by my father who all but dragged me next door. Then Dante got down on one knee and shoved a blue ring box in my face. His entire family along with mine sat in the front row seats.

While I stood there stunned, knowing Jiff was waiting for me at his families' home, I waited for Dante to ask the question. Everyone waited for me to answer. The question never came.

I was saved when Detective Hanky, Dante's previous partner, stormed through the front door announcing there were multiple homicides in progress with hostages, and Captain Deedler was needed for it…now.

Dante looked relieved when he shoved the ring in his brother's hand and ran out the house behind Hanky like he was shot out of a cannon. I followed on their heels. Had it not been for a multiple homicide that could have been my worst Christmas ever.

The two Navarre Beach police officers were staring at me waiting for an answer while I was daydreaming about the last holidays. Jiff nudged me back to the present. They had asked our names and how to reach us and took our statements. I informed the female officer taking my name and information that it appeared the lost dog was a Schnauzer, based on the special order leash embroidered with the name and breed on the dead woman's wrist.

"I do Schnauzer Rescue in New Orleans. You can Google me or find our Facebook page. Here's the number for Homicide Detective Hanky with the NOPD who will vouch for me, well, vouch for us," I said, nodded toward Jiff. I wrote Hanky's cell phone number on her notepad.

"I'll give her a call," Officer B. Frederick responded without looking up.

"Detective Hanky adopted a dog from me and I think of her as a friend. I think she still holds it against me that I date this guy," I nodded toward Jiff speaking with the other officer. "Detective Hanky is the former partner to my ex-boyfriend who is now her Captain."

"Ouch, bet that was tough. One cop in a relationship is one too many," Officer B. Frederick said without a smile, like she might be speaking from experience. There was no wedding band on her finger and she looked to be forty-something.

"So, if you find the little dog, I'd be happy to take him and try to find him a good home," I said. I told her how to find me on the internet under my non-profit rescue site and wrote down my name and number after Hanky's information on her notepad.

"Hey Bev, give her the name of the local shelter here. They might hold him a week or so if anyone brings him in," the male officer suggested. His name tag read J. Davis, and he looked half of Bev's age.

Office "Bev" Frederick wrote the name and address of the shelter on a page in her notebook, tore it out, and handed it to me.

"If someone finds him along the beach here, it's likely they might take him home. Most of the visitors along here are from out of town," she said closing her notebook.

"Whoever finds him, I just hope they love him and take care of him," I said. "Most people consider them high maintenance because they need regular grooming about every six weeks that costs about forty to forty-five bucks."

"I'll pass that along if I hear if anyone has found him or is considering keeping him. I'll give them your number to talk to, if that's okay?" she asked.

"Sure. I'm happy to help any way I can. I would hope someone would do it for me if my dog was lost," I said. I took a last look at the dead woman before the younger male officer started covering her up.

Beach Patrol, whose name "Magic Mike" was embroidered on the front of his skin-tight shirt, looked like he was about to jump in his dune buggy and ride off into what was left of the morning mist. Instead, he made his way over to us and asked our names and where we were staying.

"My name is Brandy Alexander and I'm, well we're both from New Orleans. We're here for a long weekend," I said. "We plan to leave Monday."

"Brandy Alexander, huh? From New Orleans, well that makes sense," he said without smiling. "What's your boyfriend's name, Jim Beam?"

"No, Jack Daniels. So, you're Magic Mike?" I asked.

"Hey, look, just trying to get the basics here," he said.

"My name is Jiff Heinkel and I'm a criminal defense attorney in New Orleans," Jiff said and reached to take my hand. "We're staying at the Beach Breeze Condos, number 101."

I added with the nicest voice I could, "Would you look for the Schnauzer? I think it belonged on the end of that leash the dead woman has around her wrist. I do breed rescue for them and I'll find him a good home."

Neither Jiff nor I had anything to write with so

Magic Mike pulled one of his cards from a side pocked of his baggy, knee-length shorts, an odd choice I thought with the skin-tight top. The card was laminated with just his name and phone number on it. I bet he gave these to all the girls.

"Text your info to that number and I'll call you if I find him," he said.

"He might have a collar on with the name Rascal on it," I said. "See," I pointed to the leash floating in the water just inches away from where the body remained covered. "They are a custom set people order for their pets."

"Cool," he said without looking at the leash on the woman's arm I pointed to. "I'll call you if I find him." Then he revved his ride and took off leaving the uniform police to wait for forensics, the coroner, and the crime scene investigating personnel.

"Dune buggies…riding lawnmowers with a sun roof," Jiff said more to himself than to me.

He took my hand and pulled me along back to our condo.

"You thought there wouldn't be anyone on the beach till noon," I said. "We met three new people and did a good deed finding that girl before she floated away. Maybe we'll do another and find her dog."

"Yes, and if we waited around any longer, we'd be stuck there all morning," he said. "They know where to find us. Not exactly the way I wanted to start our long weekend."

"Me neither, but I'm worried about that little dog. I'd really like to find him."

"C'mon, Brandy, I know you. You want to solve this murder and find out who killed her."

"No. I don't need to find her killer. I want to find that dog, but… if I find out who killed her along the way, well, that would be the bonus round."

"This is supposed to be a relaxing trip," Jiff said with an emphasis on 'relaxing'.

"I'm relaxing," I said. "Let's go for a ride up the beach and then we can come back and I'll make you breakfast."

"A ride up the beach?" Jiff asked. He stopped and looked at me. "You're not fooling me. You want to ride up the beach and look for that dog, don't you?"

"Well… yes, but, only for an hour or so, then I'll be satisfied."

"You won't be satisfied until we find him," Jiff said shaking his head. "I have a sunset sailing trip scheduled for six o'clock this evening," he said looking at his watch.

"Oh, we'll be back way before then," I said waving my hand at him like it was no big deal.

He let out an exaggerated breath.

"You can't be tired already," I teased. "Look, it's only seven-thirty a.m. and we've already had an adventure."

"All right. After our sunset sail this evening, I planned for us to have dinner down there on the beach.

The sailboat is at a marina near Pensacola so I thought we could have dinner at the Grand Marlin. I made a reservation for eight-thirty if that's all right with you?"

"That is perfect. All I have to do today is make a phone call," I said.

"A phone call? To who?" Jiff looked at me sideways wrinkling his forehead.

"The animal shelter to give them my name and tell them I think there's a runaway Schnauzer that might be coming their way," I said.

He just shook his head as we made our way along the water's edge heading back toward our condo.

"When we found her, I noticed her footprints in the sand near the body. If they were hers, it seemed she was walking or running toward Fort Walton. Did you see that?" I asked trying to sound as casual as I could.

"No, I didn't notice her footprints," he said.

We walked along in silence while I churned details over in my head. Things I saw on the woman's body that might give me a hint as to where she stayed or where the dog might be headed. She was wearing running shorts, a T-shirt and rubber shoes sold at a sporting goods store to walk in the sand and water.

"I wonder why the dog wasn't leashed," I mused more to myself.

"No, I didn't see her footprints." he said again with a little too much emphasis on 'her'.

"Well, what did you see?" I asked. I knew he was messing with me now. He saw or noticed something while I went off on the 911 scavenger hunt.

"Paw prints. I saw small, paw prints that looked like they were running in the opposite direction we're walking now. The tide is coming in, so they're lost but it looked like the little bugger ran that way," he said. He turned around and held his arm out pointing straight ahead.

"I can't believe you. Why didn't you tell me this sooner? This little dog might be picked up on the highway and God only knows where he could wind up. I'm always afraid someone will use them as a bait dog in a dog fighting ring. We need to find him."

"Okay, let's go get the car keys and drive around for a few minutes. Maybe we'll spot him if he made it up to the highway before a car hits him."

"Are you trying to make me crazy?" I asked.

Chapter Three

S ATURDAY AFTERNOON WE drove around for what felt like hours. We scoured the highway that separated the beach where our condo was from the residential areas on the north side of it. We drove in and out of each subdivision looking for a dog and we weren't even sure what he looked like. He could have been white, black, a party mix, a giant, or small. I prayed he still had that matching collar on.

Finally, we decided to go back to the condo and do what we came here to do, and that was relax. Jiff was going to relax, and I was going to worry about that little Schnauzer. I gathered up beach towels, beach blanket, suntan lotions ranging from two SPF all the way to fifty SPF. I stuffed that and all the miscellaneous paraphernalia I needed in my beach bag along with my Walkman and headsets.

Jiff prepared the ice chest he brought for my Pellegrino waters and his beer. He made two sandwiches and prepared some cheese and crackers he put in airtight bags. He told me he figured I would probably eat only half of one sandwich but he suspected I would definitely eat the cheese and crackers. He was right. If I had to pick on one thing to eat for the rest of my life, it would be cheese and crackers.

"It's a good thing our condo is right here at the walkway," he said as we struggled with the folding chairs, my stuff, his cooler and an umbrella. "I'll make two trips, just carry what you can."

"I've got it. We need one of those carts with dune buggy tires," I said. "They roll right over the sand with no effort."

"My brother has one of those. He hauls a pop-up tent with a floor out here, an inflatable boat he rows around in, every inflatable toy, ring, or float made for the water. He also brings along a foot pump," he said and stopped to swap hands with what he was carrying. Then he went on mentioning more things his brother lugged out here. "He brings several noodles, a volleyball net, and volleyball, football, you name it."

"Why didn't we ask him to come with us? We wouldn't be carrying any of this stuff," I said making Jiff smile.

"His girlfriend doesn't like sand on her feet. That's why he brings the tent with a floor in it."

"Why doesn't she just stay by the pool?"

"Because, she loves the beach."

"Just the beach? No sand? Isn't that what a beach is? Sand?" I asked.

"He carries her piggyback from the walkway to the tent, then from the tent to the water and back," he said.

"It seems some of the Heinkel men know how to treat their women," I said. "Why do I have to carry all my own stuff like a pack mule…and walk across the sand?" I made a face with my mouth turned down and my eyes squinting like I was about to cry.

"That's it. I'm buying one of those carts for our next trip," he said.

That's good, I thought. *Finding a dead body on the beach didn't put him off planning future trips with me or coming back to the beach together.*

It took us several minutes to decide exactly where to make our beach camp. Too close to the water and the tide could get us. Too far away and we had to walk over hot sand without our shoes to take a dip. Finally, I took two steps closer to the water and said, "Here," and put my stuff down. Jiff agreed it was the perfect spot.

He took forever digging a hole to set up the umbrella saying he was worried a good puff (his term for breeze) would pick it up and propel it down the beach. He buried it so deep the only people who could have walked upright under it was Pygmies. I had to open my lounge chair and carry it bent over at the waist to set it up and sit in it. It would take a category five hurricane "puff" to upend this thing and send it flying.

Once we both had crawled into our chairs under the umbrella, I opened the cooler to spread out the lunch he made for our beach picnic.

"Is this your brother's umbrella you talked about?" I asked Jiff as he popped open another beer.

"Yes, isn't it great?" he said and handed me the baggie with the cheese and crackers.

"What time is our sailing trip?" I asked. "We need to give ourselves time to pick up what we brought, get back, shower and get ready."

"We need to arrive by six p.m. We should shower together to save time, so we can stay out here longer," he said. I could see him looking at me out of the corner of his sunglasses.

"Good idea," I said.

WE WERE GOING to meet the catamaran that Jiff booked us on at the marina in Pensacola. As we made our way down a pier to the far end, we passed all types and sizes of sailboats.

"How do you know which one we are looking for?" I asked Jiff. "Do you have a name?"

"No, I don't have a name but I bet you it's the biggest catamaran out here. Look for one that's seventy-seven feet long."

"Seventy-seven feet? How did they get it in here?" I asked.

I've done some sailing with friends on Lake Pontchartrain and even contemplated buying a sailboat. I took lessons at the yacht club but soon realized how much upkeep a boat is and I wanted someone to sail off into the sunset with. I was tired of doing things by myself after years of waiting on and dating Dante, my childhood sweetheart, only to be abandoned on more dates than we ever had.

"I think that's it docked at the end of the pier. This marina doesn't have a slip big enough for it," Jiff said. "The Captain I booked this cruise with said he's on his way down to the Caymans or the B.V.I. from here."

"Wow!" I said when I spotted it. It was a magnificent sailboat, and it was big, really, really big. It was by far the biggest yacht I had ever seen, let alone was about to have the pleasure of an evening cruise on. Painted on the port, aft side of the hull was the name, *In Your Dreams 77*. The seventy-seven stood for her length…seventy-seven feet long. She had a wide cockpit with dual helms and the bow had super wide trampolines between the two hulls for sunbathing or relaxing. Even at my first look this yacht screamed luxury on top of luxury. The fly bridge and the bow off the salon had blue canvas awnings to enjoy shade while being on deck. From the main deck there were three-hundred-sixty-degree views no matter where you stood inside or outside.

"Gosh, it looks like we're the first ones here. Do you know how many others are going on this sunset cruise?" I asked Jiff.

"No one else," he said and shouted to the captain for permission to come aboard.

A nice-looking man, about Jiff's height and age appeared from the upper deck. He was wearing a white polo shirt with the yacht's name and his, Captain

Daniel Becnel.

"Hey, you're right on time. Welcome aboard. I'm Daniel," he said offering his hand to me as I stepped onto the deck from the pier. He turned to Jiff and said, "Good seeing you, man. It's been awhile." After we boarded, Jiff introduced me.

"Take a look around and make yourself at home. I have to call in our sail plan to the coast guard," Daniel said. "Just a precaution and safety policy."

"I can't believe we have this entire cruise to ourselves," I said to Jiff.

Jiff told me he liked having the yacht all to ourselves because it would be quiet and we could enjoy a peaceful sail.

"I've been on cruises where someone talks non-stop and doesn't listen to the sound of why we're out here in the first place," he said.

"Amen to that," our Captain said and told me to call him Daniel. "Make yourselves at home. I believe you both are sailors, right?"

"That's a yes, if you mean, do I know the front end of the boat from the back end?" I said.

"Well, I might ask you to lend a hand here or there with the lines casting off and when we return to dock, but otherwise, enjoy yourself. Wine and beer are in the galley below," he said.

Right about then, a little gray dog came out of the salon barking at us. I was thunderstruck at it being a Schnauzer.

"Well, look who's finally awake," Daniel said and the little dog wagged his tail for a split second, then went back to barking at us.

I knelt and put out my hand to make friends. After he sniffed his approval of me he went back to barking at Jiff until he put his hand down for the little guy to sniff.

"Yeah, he's been napping ever since we got back here from my supply run."

While I stared at the little dog, Jiff told Daniel by way of explanation that we each had a Schnauzer and I did rescue for that breed.

"What a coincidence that we all have the same breed dog," Jiff said.

"He's not my dog," Daniel said. "I found him running along the beach this morning when I went into Navarre to pick up some engine parts for my BVI trip."

"Where did you find him?" I asked him.

"In the supply store's parking lot. He just fell down in front of me he was so exhausted. I picked him and brought him here and gave him some food and water," Daniel said.

"Did you call the shelters nearby to see if anyone is trying to find him?" I asked.

"No. I haven't had time since I've been getting ready to leave tomorrow and for this evening's sail with you folks."

By now, the dog had put his paws on the leg I was kneeling on, and I got a good look at the collar. I thought I was so preoccupied with wanting to find that little Schnauzer from this morning that my eyes were making me believe the name I was seeing on his collar was Rascal.

"Jiff, look at this," I said.

"Wow, this little guy just won the doggie lottery," Jiff said.

"I was going to post a picture of him on Facebook to see if anyone was looking for him," Daniel said adjusting a sail to pick up a little speed.

"I didn't even think of posting on Facebook to look for him," I said looking up at Jiff. Then I said to Daniel, "I think we know who owns this dog and you won't believe how our day started."

"Or how fortuitous it was scheduling this cruise with you," added Jiff. "You have saved me from scouring the coast for this little dog over the next two days we're here on vacation."

"Rascal's the name on his collar," said Daniel. "He seems to respond to it."

After Jiff and I helped cast off and when we were clear of the harbor, Jiff gave Daniel the story of our early morning beach stroll resulting in finding Rascal's owner. I decided to go below and grab us beers, wine or whatever we wanted. I walked through double sliding marine glass doors to the salon with Rascal at my heels. He followed me everywhere. I wondered if this dog knew how to swim. I stopped worrying when I saw how good his sea legs were.

The salon was crafted in a subtle mix of teak and light woods with cream colored sofas and oversized chairs for an organic feel. To the left was the galley that opened to the dining area on the other side. It had one long counter, bar height, with five bar stools. This open area was ample entertainment space to lounge and relax in for the ten guests this yacht slept, with enough room for a heck of a party.

At the other side of the banquet style dining area, double wide sliding doors opened onto the bow under an awning with more outdoor dining and modular seating. This gave new meaning to the term open floor plan. It reminded me of a lanai design you see in Hawaii. Besides the banquet tables, there were built-in sofa-type seats along the gunwales. You could host a party on the bow end with more people than I could fit into my apartment.

The galley was nicer than my parents' kitchen and they had recently remodeled it with Viking appliances. This had a five-burner stove, dual sinks, expansive work space and a glass front refrigerator. It was stocked with cheeses, wine, Pellegrino waters and every name brand beer you have ever heard of.

When I saw the other refrigerator with the stainless door, I realized the glass front one was a wine cooler. They were both the same twenty cubic inch size. A tray with cheese, fruit, crackers and cocktail napkins was out on the counter next to the wine bucket icing a bottle of Dom Perignon. Another ice bucket in the sink was chilling two champagne flutes.

"Hey, Miss Blondie Rescue," Daniel's voice and face popped up on a small screen in the galley. He was up on the bridge at the wheel. "Please bring out a couple of beers and remove the plastic cover on that cheese tray I took all afternoon preparing for you." The cheese tray was the ready-made type on a black tray with a clear plastic dome cover you pick up at grocery stores.

Jiff started laughing, and I also heard him suggest Daniel call me Brandy.

I helped myself to a slice of what looked like white cheddar and broke off a bite to give Rascal. Now, he would love me forever.

Rascal followed me and Jiff met us to help me carry the tray and drinks to the deck up top. Just when I was about to pick up Rascal he managed to climb up the stairs following the cheese tray.

"Is it safe up here for him" I asked Daniel handing him one of the beers I selected.

"Oh yeah. We're not heading into anything rough. This is going to be a smooth sail. except for the wind in your face, you won't even know we're moving."

"Then we won't spill our drinks," Jiff said.

Rascal jumped up on a cushioned seat and watched us. He looked from person to person when we spoke.

"Too bad this isn't the life for a dog, cuz I'd love the companionship. I'd like to take him along with me," Daniel said. "But there are days, sometimes weeks at a time he won't set foot on land."

"Dogs are adaptable and Schnauzers are smart. They will learn whatever you take the time to teach them," I said. "But I will find him a perfect home, if that's what you're worried about."

"She will," Jiff added. "This is the only breed she rescues, so she gives them her undivided attention." He sounded so proud of me when he said it.

"Thanks. I think I'm already attached to the little guy," Daniel said. "I can't believe you two found his owner just this morning. Cops have any leads?"

"We didn't hang around, but I got the name of a policewoman and a Beach Patrol dude that showed up. I was going to call him tomorrow to see if he found Rascal. He said he would keep looking for him when he was on patrol," I said.

"Do you remember that guy's name, the beach patrol guy?" Daniel asked.

"How could I forget? The name on his shirt was Magic Mike," I said.

Daniel laughed. "That guy's undercover, but don't tell him or anyone else I said that. He'd kill me and don't count on him helping look for this or any other dog."

"Who are we gonna tell?" asked Jiff.

"How did you meet him?" I asked.

"Probably at a bar around here somewhere. There's a great Tiki bar overlooking the gulf in Destin," he said to us. "In fact, I saw Mike this morning at the West

Marine Boat Supply when I went to pick up parts. They've been working a case along here, and he won't tell me what's involved. I think he said he was Special Forces. Those guys keep mostly to themselves—not exactly party animals. The name is to make you think he's the lifeguard type."

"The name's working for him," Jiff said and nodded at me.

The cruise lasted an hour longer than planned and I found out Jiff and Daniel had somewhat of a history together. They knew each other from law school. Daniel decided he had had it with the corporate world in America. After a big case he settled, he checked out, and bought this rig. He charters it to people, mostly Europeans, a week to six months at a time taking them anywhere in the world they want to go. Not bad.

While Jiff and Daniel were commiserating on law school, professors and their time spent there, I went to get another beer for Daniel and get champagne refills for me and Jiff. Rascal followed me. Cheese will do it every time. While I looked for the same beer Daniel was drinking, I noticed Rascal was scratching at his collar again. I saw him doing it a few times when we were up on deck.

I checked to see if it was too tight. I could barely get a finger between it and his skin so I loosened it. It was then I noticed the underside of his collar was lumpy. A piece of gross grain ribbon matching the color of his collar was stitched to hold the lumpy something in there. I pulled at the stitching and a sort of sleeve peeled off in my hand. Each end was stitched and I could feel something flat and rectangular-shaped inside that slide around. It felt like four different flat and rectangular somethings. I needed a ripping tool you use for sewing or scissors to open the sleeve and decided I'd do it later back at the condo with Jiff. I didn't want to drag Daniel into more than he already bargained for, especially since he said he had plans to leave in the morning.

I put the sleeve from Rascal's collar in my purse and planned to talk to Jiff about it later when I could open it and see what it hid. The sleeve and the dead girl seemed all too connected. I fit the collar back on Rascal and brought the beer up to Daniel.

"We're going to the Grand Marlin after this. Do you want to join us?" Jiff was asking when I handed Daniel the beer.

"You really want me to tag along? I might try talking your pretty girlfriend here into sailing off into the sunset with me," Daniel said. "She seems to know her way around sailboats."

"I don't think it would take much to convince me," I said and Jiff gave me his hurt puppy dog face.

"What are you going to do with Rascal?" Daniel asked. "I can watch him here until you finish dinner and you can come pick him up on your way back to your condo. If you call me when you are on your way, I'll even walk him to the end of the pier."

"Deal," Jiff and I answered together.

Chapter Four

THE GRAND MARLIN overlooked Pensacola Bay. There was a restaurant inside, but we sat outside, in the bar area at a dining table. There was a one-man band playing an acoustic guitar or changing to a piano keyboard at one end of the outdoor area. The ceiling height had to be forty feet and the breeze off the bay felt like we were sitting somewhere at a really nice restaurant on an island in the Caribbean. The menu was, indeed, grand. I had a lobster appetizer that was perfect, and I ordered it as my whole meal. Jiff had fish of the day, a grilled Mahi Mahi that was marinated in rum and spices. He said it was the best he had ever eaten.

We finished our glass of wine and watched as ferries picked up people from the pier connected to the restaurant and shuttled them back to one of the five tower high-rise developments about a mile away. Maybe four to ten people would embark on the ferry each way. For a Saturday night there wasn't much traffic. The lights at both ends of their destination had come on twinkling to welcome the ferry's arrival and to light the way for guests to make their way up to the restaurant.

On our way back to the marina I was tempted to tell Jiff what I found on Rascal's collar that might have something to do with the owner being killed. The fact was, I was afraid to see what it was. Now, this had escalated from finding a home for a little rescue abandoned by a bad situation to finding out what was inside that collar and what it might lead to.

My skin had that creepy crawly sensation every time I thought about what might be inside that dog's collar. I did not want this to derail the remainder of our long weekend Jiff planned, but the sleeve was distracting me and my mind kept going back to it. I kept wondering what it was going to tell us. I couldn't wait to get back to the condo to open it. I kept thinking I should tell him sooner rather than later, but there was something I just could not put my finger on as to why I was procrastinating. I convinced myself it would keep, and I didn't want to ruin our pleasant evening here at this marvelous restaurant.

When we pulled into the marina parking lot, we saw Daniel standing at the end of the pier as planned. While Jiff looked for a parking place, a van ahead of us stopped in front of Daniel. Two guys got out and tried to take Rascal away from him. One guy was trying to pick up Rascal, but Rascal was snapping and maneuvering away from him.

Daniel was trying to talk to the bigger guy while

the smaller man was trying to grab Rascal. The little dog was faring better by outmaneuvering his assailant than Daniel was. The two men looked menacing and were acting aggressive toward Daniel and the dog.

"Brandy, get down," Jiff said slamming on the brakes. He jumped out of our car yelling, "Stop! Police!" at the two men. He flipped open his wallet and held up his hand like he was showing a badge or something.

The big guy punched Daniel knocking him down to the pier and pointed a gun at Jiff. He was about to fire a shot when Daniel did a sweep with his foot and knocked the guy off his feet. Then Daniel pushed Rascal in the water with his other foot.

The big guy let out a stream of expletives as he got up. The smaller guy who was trying to chase Rascal down kicked Daniel hard in the mid-section and they both jumped back in the van and took off.

"We ran toward Daniel and Jiff went to help him while I looked around in the water for Rascal. He was dog paddling his little heart out toward a boat a few slips away. I called to him. He turned and started paddling back toward me. A couple came off their boat to see what was causing all the commotion. I was lying flat on the pier trying to reach Rascal but he was about one foot too far away.

"I'll go in after him," I said as I stood up and kicked off my shoes. I ran onto a large sailboat near where Rascal was swimming toward. Its keel probably had at least a five-foot draw so I figured the water in the harbor was six to eight feet, definitely over my head. From the transom I did a giant stride into the water and Rascal swam right up to me. I held him away from me with one arm while I tread water with my other arm and legs. I worked my way back to where Daniel and Jiff were standing on the pier joined by the couple who came out to see what was going on.

"Wait," the man said as Jiff tried to lean down to get Rascal but was about a foot short of reaching him like I had been. I couldn't lift him out of the water high enough. "I have a net. I think we can scoop him up in it."

"You didn't even get your hair wet," the woman said. We waited for the man to return with the net while I held Rascal and bobbed in the water.

"I took a Life Saving/First Aid class for water related sports and they teach you how to jump in and keep your head above water so you can keep an eye on the person, or in this case, dog, needing help," I said. A boat passed in the marina and sent a gentle wake my way. Rascal and I bobbed with the wave.

The lady nodded and said, "That was impressive."

When the man got back with the net, Jiff was flat on the pier reaching for Rascal while I pushed him toward Jiff. The man scooped his net under him and I pushed the rim of the net until Jiff grabbed it and Rascal. The man helped raise the other end of the net by the pole so Jiff could hang on to Rascal in the scoop and keep him from falling out of the net back into the water.

Jiff reached down for me, pulling me up by one arm and I twisted so I could land sitting on the pier.

Once we were out of the water, everyone, except for me, all stepped back so we didn't get sprayed when Rascal shook several times. The woman had gone to get us a towel so both of us could dry off.

"I'll try to get this back to you tomorrow," I told her.

"Don't worry about it. It's an old towel. It's the least we can do for the little guy and you. He's had quite an adventure," she said. "If you need anything else, we'll be up a while."

Jiff and her husband helped Daniel to his feet. Then, they went back to their sailboat and their cocktails.

"Whatever made you yell Police!" Daniel asked Jiff.

"Because I've never seen anyone on TV run away from someone yelling Lawyer!" he said. "I have a badge that says I'm an officer of the court. From a distance it might pass for a badge."

"That was fast thinking. Daniel, so was that sweep on that big guy when you got a chance," I said.

"What do you think this was all about? Dognapping?" Daniel asked as he started to hobble back to the catamaran with Jiff's help.

"Do you want to go to an emergency room? Maybe something's broken," I said.

"Nah, nothing feels broken. I'm only bruised, and that's mostly my ego," Daniel said.

"Do you think we need to report this to the police?" I asked.

"Did anyone get the license plate? And even if you did, that van is probably stolen," Daniel said as he limped along. "That big guy I knocked down had a tat on his forearm. I'm not sure what it was, but it was ugly, black and didn't have a good shape or design to it."

"A prison tat?" Jiff asked. "Do you know what those look like when they do it themselves?"

"I don't know, but it looks like it could have been self-inflicted. It didn't look like a professional job," Daniel moaned as tried to step up and onto the boarding plank.

"Don't you think we should go to our condo? If those two come back, they will be looking for Daniel because they saw you with the dog," I said. "This way, we can get you back here early and both you and Rascal will be safe with us tonight. If you change your mind about needing an emergency room, we can take you."

"No Emergency Room. Nothing's broken. I'm bruised but nothing's broken. Even if a rib is broken, there's nothing they can do that I can't do," he said and when he tried to smile at me, he winced.

"Okay, tough guy," I said. "Tell me what to do and I'll go lock up for you while Jiff helps you get in the car."

"Oh, God, I think I love this woman," Daniel said from the back seat as Jiff helped him in and I pushed Rascal in next to him.

Daniel gave me the keys to lock up the controls and the salon and said to leave all the lights on so if anyone did board, someone would see them. On my way back to his boat, I stopped by the couple's boat who helped us and asked if they would call the harbormaster and report what happened.

I told them where to find me and gave them our cell numbers. The husband said he had a lock and chain to put it through the gate leading onto the pier. That would slow them down if they came back. I told them Daniel wanted me to leave all the lights on in case anyone boarded so they might be able to see them and call the police.

The couple said they would keep an eye on things until Daniel got back. I got back to the car, Jiff drove all of us, Daniel, Rascal, and me back to our condo.

🐈 🐈 🐈 🐈 🐈 🐈 🐈 🐈 🐈 🐈

JIFF TOOK DANIEL up to the condo to get him settled in a guest room while I walked Rascal. He was dry by now. I was still damp. Daniel had made a leash out of sail ties, webbing strips used to tie the mainsail to the boom. I had to smile at the invention. Sailors were practical and innovative when it came to making one thing work as something else.

A couple was walking a little black dog that looked

like he had some Schnauzer in his family tree. The woman stopped me and said, "Be careful with your dog. Two men stopped here earlier asking if this was our dog or did we find him. They said they lost a Schnauzer. Isn't that what your dog is?"

"Yes, he's a Schnauzer. What did they look like? Do you know what kind of car they were in?" I asked.

"There were two rough looking guys, about thirty, forty maybe. They were in a white van. They didn't get out of the car. Two white guys. One had long, dark hair to his collar pushed behind his ears. He had on a dark blue T-shirt, I think. It was a dark looking shirt, not a hoodie. The other one wore a camouflage baseball cap. I really didn't get a good look at the one in the cap since he was on the far side of the van and it was getting dark," the woman said. The husband nodded at everything she told me.

"That's a little scary," I said. If she only knew those two just beat up our friend. "Do you remember what time it was?"

"I want to say it was about eight o'clock since that's the time we usually take Buttons for his evening walk. I didn't get the plates because they pulled up behind us and asked about Buttons here. He started growling, and we knew these two were bad news. We walked off and headed back around the building so they couldn't follow us. I guess they drove off," the man answered. "I didn't see their van parked anywhere."

"Thanks for the warning," I said. "I'll be careful."

I didn't let Rascal dilly dally on his walk. We made our way back to the condo and as soon as I saw Daniel and Jiff all three of us said, at the same time, "You won't believe what I found out."

"You first," I said.

"Daniel called Mike. Remember the beach patrol guy from this morning?" Jiff said.

I nodded.

"Those mutts who attacked me were in a stolen vehicle," Daniel said. "Mike said the police identified the dead woman from a call that came in. Her sister reported her and the dog missing when they didn't come back from a morning walk. She had a photo with her and sure enough, it was her sister."

Jiff couldn't wait to add, "They also got some skin and blood from under the woman's fingernails. They might be able to ID whoever attacked her if they are in the system. I told Mike about the two who jumped Daniel with one having a prison-looking tat so maybe they'll get a hit. They're running it through the national database but that takes time," Jiff said. "What did you find out on your walk?"

"This man and his wife stopped me and said two guys in a white van came through the parking lot earlier, around eight p.m., and asked if they found the little dog they were walking. It's about Rascal's size but he was a mix and black," I said. "That means those two in the white van the couple saw here, are the same two who attacked Daniel. They also might be who killed that girl. It all seems too connected."

"I wonder how they made the connection from looking here to me in Pensacola," Daniel said. "Seems odd."

We all agreed. It was getting late and we all felt worn out, so we said good night.

As soon as I entered the master suite from the bathroom, Jiff said, "Out with it. What do you have?"

"How do you know I have something?"

"Because you have been fidgeting with something in your pocketbook since we left the dock. You keep checking to make sure it's still there and you've kept it in your lap all through dinner," he said. "I'm usually the one looking out for the whereabouts of your pocketbook when we go out."

The only two people in the world who still called a ladies' purse a pocketbook were Jiff and my Dad.

"I didn't want to tell you at dinner and spoil such a beautiful evening we were having. I was going to tell you when we got back… and after, you know… after… later, after we got back here."

"Well, we're back. What do you have that's got you so nervous?"

"I really don't know what I have. I didn't open it. I saw Rascal kept scratching at his collar when I went down to get more drinks on Daniel's boat, so I took it off him to adjust it. That's when I found a sleeve of something sewn on the inside of it," I said. showing him what I had in my purse all evening. "I thought we should see what it is together."

"I can't believe you kept this from me all evening," he said and took the sleeve from me to look at. He rolled it between his fingers moving what was inside back and forth.

"You should be glad I found it and took it off his collar, whatever it is. What if those guys got him, or what if whatever it is shouldn't get wet? After all, Rascal just went for a swim," I said.

"Good point," he said. "It's probably best if we didn't drag Daniel into this since he wants to leave tomorrow."

"That's what I was thinking and why I waited until we were alone to show you. How well do you know Daniel?" I asked.

"I've known him since law school. We were in the same classes and a study group together which was the sum total of my social life back then. We weren't, aren't, close friends. I'd bump into him at the courthouse once in a while after we were admitted to the Bar," Jiff said and looked up at me. "Why do you ask that?"

"I'm not sure why. I need to think about it some more," I said.

"C'mon Brandy, let's see what was inside Rascal's collar," Jiff said.

Chapter Five

AFTER FINDING SCISSORS and cutting one end of the thread loose on the sleeve, one end of the strip opened and out fell four flash drives. All that was marked on them was the number one through four.

"We need a computer to see what's on them," Jiff said.

"I didn't bring my laptop," I said. "I usually drag it along everywhere I go and never use it. Now that I need it, I don't have it."

"I didn't bring mine either," Jiff said.

"Wow, you really planned for us to disconnect from the grid for the whole weekend, didn't you?" I said. "No laptop… impressive. So, how are we going to find out what's on these?" I picked up one of the drives turning it over and inspecting it. I said it more to myself than a verbal question.

"When we go back to Daniel's yacht we could take a look at them on his computer," Jiff said.

"Then we're involving Daniel and we don't know how much is on these drives, or even what it is. It could take time," I said looking at them closely. There were no markings on them other than the numbers one through four.

"Or we could call Beach Patrol, tell him what we found and ask him to bring his computer here to see what's on these," Jiff said.

"If that guy is working on some case here, he's gonna take them, and not let us see what's on any of it," I said. "He's so rude and unfriendly, he might even arrest us for having them. You heard what Daniel said about him calling us about Rascal."

"They could be encrypted and take a while to figure out." Jiff said. "If they are, then we will need Mike to see what's on them."

"Look, as soon as he hears that we found these, we're out," I said and crawled onto Jiff's lap facing him. It didn't take much investigating on his part to see I had nothing on under my robe.

"Let's go to bed, we have all day tomorrow to work on finding a computer," he said.

THE ALARM CLOCK said five a.m. Daniel was already in the kitchen trying to make coffee quietly, but the inviting smell came wafting in like a bugle blowing revelry to me. I also pop awake when the sun comes up. Light was coming in through the windows. Jiff, on the other hand, was still sleeping like he had been drugged. He had pulled a pillow over his face to block out the light. The sun coming in from the sliding glass doors that lead to the balcony off of our bedroom lit up the room like Hollywood, yet he slept on.

Slipping into some shorts and a T-shirt, I quietly left and closed the bedroom door. A cup of steaming black coffee sat next to Daniel while he looked and scrolled through his cell phone.

"Well, even if it is a Sunday, I'm glad to see another early riser like myself," I said. "One who even makes coffee!"

"Where's Jiff? Is he awake?" Daniel asked.

"Not quite. What time did you want to get to the marina?" I asked.

"Thirty minutes ago," he said and smiled. "Take your time but see if you can get him going. My side where that goofball kicked me hurts more this morning than it did last night. I'm not moving so fast."

"It hurts more this morning because you had the benefit of several medicinal beers last night," I said. "I'll bring him a cup of coffee. The smell of this should get him going."

I went back to our bedroom and Jiff was sitting up in bed, not really awake. He was thinking about it, I could tell.

"I heard you two in the kitchen," he mumbled.

"Sorry, we were trying to be quiet. I brought you some coffee if that will help." I handed the mug to him. Jiff sat there holding it with his eyes closed.

"C'mon, Daniel can't drive himself to his boat and get the car back to us," I said.

"Tell him to call Uber," Jiff said.

"You don't mean that. Look at how nice an evening we had with him until the gangsters showed up. We can't ask him to call Uber," I said. "Besides, what if they're waiting for him back at the marina?"

"Another reason he should call Uber. He found the dog and brought it to his boat," Jiff said. "We're helping him out by taking the dog off his boat, and off his hands."

"Where's the dog?" I asked suddenly and ran back to the kitchen. "Daniel, where's Rascal?"

"I tried to take him for a walk when I got up but he didn't want to get out of bed. He's still sleeping in my room," he said.

"Well, we'll walk him when we leave unless he gets up before then. I don't have any dog food here for him so we'll have to get him some on our way home," I said.

"Give him cereal or eggs. That's what I fed him and he liked it," Daniel said.

"That's because he was probably starving from not eating all day. This breed loves food, so they will eat just about anything, even stuff that's not good for them."

"So, tell me. How did you two get together?" Daniel asked changing the subject.

"How well do you know him?" I asked changing it back on him.

"We met in a law school study group. We didn't know each other from high school or from the same neighborhood. We both made law review so often saw each other at the same functions but we really didn't socialize. He's a smart guy," Daniel said.

"Yes, he's smart, but I'm wondering what type of girls he dated?"

"I never saw him with a date during law school. Girls seemed interested in him, he's good looking, but I don't think I ever saw him with anyone, now that I think about it. My take on him is he didn't suffer the kind of gal that was forward or threw herself at him. So how did you two meet?"

"At a Mardi Gras parade. He stopped in the middle of Lee Circle with the men's marching group he was with and looked at me. I left who I was standing with, walked right up to him and kissed him. He never said a word to me until the police started to move him along, then he asked me to meet him at the end of the parade," I said.

"I'm guessing you met him at the end of that parade?" Daniel asked smiling.

"Yes, I found him after the parade without even knowing his name," I said. I really didn't want to get into how I went to meet him after the parade, watched him get shot, then whisked off in an ambulance and the adventure that followed. Daniel didn't need to know all of it, how I found him after that kiss, and the shooting. "You know we both have a dog like Rascal. Jiff said he saw me when I brought a rescue to his doorman in his building. He saw me before I ever saw him."

"Uh huh," was all Daniel said. "Let's see if we can get Rip Van Winkle and his dog, Rascal Van Winkle, up and at 'em."

Jiff was standing in the bedroom, dressed in khaki shorts with a belt, a white polo shirt, and Sperry topsiders. He still held the full mug of coffee. I wondered if he ever put it down to get dressed. Rascal had moved from Daniel's room to the warm spot where Jiff had been sitting.

"C'mon you two," I said. "Time to go and get this guy back to his boat so he can shove off and we can go to work."

Chapter Six

EVERYTHING AT THE marina looked calm and quiet when we pulled up but I got that creepy-crawly feeling all over my skin again. Something was off. Jiff and I decided to leave Rascal at the condo in case we ran into the same guys. If they didn't see the dog, they might not bother us since last night was dark and we didn't think they got a good look at us.

There was a young woman, thirty-something, waiting on the pier near Daniel's sailboat. She had that long, thin super model look about her with shoulder length brunette hair. Everything about her screamed high maintenance. As we approached, I could see she had been crying. Her eyes were red, and she held a tissue crumbled up in the palm of her hand. Even with red eyes she was still glamourous, and I'd kill to know what kind of makeup she used that didn't smear or smudge.

"Excuse me," she said when she saw us heading for the boat. "Are you the people who found Rascal?"

The three of us just looked at each other and said nothing. When I looked at her, I realized she looked very much like the woman we found dead on the beach yesterday morning.

"Who are you?" I asked.

"I'm, Rascal's owner. My name is," she dabbed at her eyes and cleared her throat. "Ashley Westlake. Rascal was really my sister's dog. Her name was Abigale Westlake… Abby, we called her Abby."

"Take your time," Daniel said, walking over to stand closer to her. He put his hand on her shoulder.

"I called the police to report my sister and her dog missing. I spoke to an officer who answered the phone and he said he worked the scene where my sister was found. He told me two people were trying to find Rascal to keep him safe. Then he told me someone called in a mugging here last night. He said the muggers were trying to steal a dog named Rascal. I knew it had to be… my sister's dog."

"Why are you so sure?" I asked. She seemed to choose her words carefully when she spoke.

"Because not many people would send someone to mug you to get her dog back. That would be my sister's ex-husband. She is… sorry, she was… recently divorced. The ex-husband she recently divorced put all their money in offshore accounts so he wouldn't have to give her anything in a settlement," she said. She started dabbing at her eyes with the balled-up tissue. "She drove here from New York with the dog two days ago. Rascal and her clothes are all she left with."

"Well, if you can prove in some way, it was your

sister's dog, I'd be happy to give him to you." I said.

"Oh, no, it's not that. I just want to make sure he gets to a safe place and a good home. You look like nice people. My sister drove here with no job, and no place to stay. She couldn't afford to take care of Rascal but she was never going to leave him with her ex. He was abusive to her, and she was sure he would hurt or kill the dog just to make her more miserable. She wanted to get as far away from him as possible and then get Rascal to a rescue group so he could never get his hands on the little guy."

"You're in luck," Daniel said nodding toward me. "This gal runs a rescue group, and she lives in New Orleans. She's just here on vacation. She'll get Rascal as far away from here as possible. You know, I'm really the one who found him…"

I cut Daniel off before he started to make out he was the hero and tried to get her phone number.

"Are you sure you don't want to keep your sister's dog?" I asked. Some people wanted to keep a pet as a last connection to a loved one. I got a lot of dogs in rescue whose owners couldn't wait to get rid of their spouse's dog or dogs. One man called me hours after his wife died and he wanted to bring me her two Schnauzers right then and there. "I'm guessing the police told you what happened to her?" I asked.

"Yes. I had to ID her late yesterday afternoon. Her ex-husband killed her or had her killed. I know he did. He's a ruthless man," she said and started crying again.

Daniel moved a tad closer and put his arm around her. "I can't keep the dog," she continued. "I travel for work and I really don't have the money to hire someone to watch him when I'm gone."

"I have to ask, but does your sister's husband have any claim on the dog? Is he a joint owner or was he the owner before your sister?" I asked.

"No. My sister bought that dog over three years ago. I don't want to have to deal with her ex if he thinks he should get the dog back," she said She tried to unfold and refold the tissue which was way past the point of being useful.

"He has a microchip in him. It's registered to my sister… Abby. She's had Rascal even before they got married. They were together only two years when she suspected he was cheating on her. Over the last year she caught him with young girls, really young girls," she said and then added, "more than once."

"Come aboard and we'll write up a paper for you to sign surrendering him to my rescue. I just hope your sister didn't add her ex to the registration," I said. "Otherwise we can't have the chip moved into our name. When I call the company to do it, they will call your sister's ex and tell him where the dog is."

"My sister was worried about that. When she got here, to Florida, to my house two days ago, she called and added my name to Rascal's microchip registration so only I could make changes if anything happened to her. At that time, she checked with the company and his name was never on it. I guess she had a premonition," Ashley said looking down at her perfectly polished hands that were still molesting the tissue. "That same day we went to an attorney, and she made out a new will leaving what little she had left or owned to me. I also have a Power of Attorney to act on her behalf."

"Okay, let's go on board and if Daniel gives us a piece of paper and a pen, I'll get you to write a surrender of Rascal over to Schnauzer Rescue," I said.

Jiff had remained quiet through the entire conversation with Ashley. Once we were all onboard, he asked her if she had a driver's license or some form of ID that we could use in case anyone came questioning my intentions.

She produced a New York driver's license of Abby Westlake and her Florida ID card that had her name, Ashley Westlake on it. There were poor quality photos on the IDs and it was hard to tell whether or not it was this woman on either of them. Florida and New York take equally bad photos for a driver's license.

Jiff took a photo of both which his cell phone and sent them to me.

"I have a Schnauzer too. In fact, both Brandy and I have Schnauzers. Is there anything in particular you can tell Brandy about Rascal? It would be good to know if he does something unusual, like hates cats or isn't good with kids. It might be helpful finding the right home for him."

I put a hand in my pocket and felt the sleeve with the flash drives. I wondered if that was the 'anything in particular' Jiff was alluding to. If this was as important as we thought it might be, why didn't she and the sister put it in a safe deposit box at a bank, I wondered.

She shook her head as the tears started again. "He is a playful, sweet dog. He seems to get along with everyone. That's all I know," she said.

"Is he neutered? We'll get that done because all dogs in rescue must be before we place them in another home," I said.

"He already is," Ashley said and wrote out she was surrendering the dog she co-owned with her deceased sister over to rescue. She signed it A. Westlake, dated it, and I asked her to write in her address here in Florida in case I needed to contact her for anything.

For a moment she looked flustered and said she'd rather not if this paper ever got into the hands of her sister's ex-husband he would know where to find her. She hurriedly finished writing in her sister's Brooklyn, New York address. She gave me her cell phone number which I put into my cell phone. I added that it was very unlikely I'd have to call her for anything but this way, no one had the number but me.

Jiff and I walked her back down the pier to her car. Ashley gave us all of Rascal's earthly belongings—his numerous dog toys, a bed, a blanket-type sofa cover, an old collar that had some vet tags and a microchip tag. She said this was all her sister brought with her when she drove down to Florida. She hoped it might help Rascal transition to his new home.

"I hope this helps with shots or anything else he needs," she said putting two one hundred-dollar bills in my hand. Then she opened her car door to leave.

"One last question," I said.

"What is your sister's ex-husband's name?" I asked. "I'd like to know in case he manages to track me down. You made him sound… resourceful."

"His name is Donnato Neglio."

Jiff and I exchanged a quick glance.

"His name sounds familiar," I said.

"He's Italian," she said. "And from New York. He's in the news from time to time, never for anything good."

"There were a couple of guys who came around looking for Rascal," Jiff said.

"Whatever you do, don't give them that dog," she said and looked very alarmed. She turned the key in the ignition, thanked us, and said she hoped we could find Rascal a good home. "He's really a great dog," she said tearing up, and then she sped out of the marina parking lot.

"It seemed like she was in a big hurry there at the end, don't you think?" I asked Jiff.

"She didn't ask about those two guys and she didn't seem surprised that they were looking for Rascal," Jiff answered. "I wonder what she didn't tell us along with the flash drives she didn't mention. Speaking of a big hurry, I bet Daniel is anxious to get underway. He said he wanted to leave early and I don't want to detain him back any longer. We still have to look at those drives and decide who to give them to."

I put my hand on Jiff's arm to keep him there a minute longer as I watched Ashley's car driving away. "Let's just make sure no one is following her," I said, and we watched her turn out the marina parking lot. We lost her for about a block before we saw her car turn onto Highway 98 eastbound. We didn't see any other cars turn in after her or look like they might be following, so we headed back to help Daniel and say goodbye.

"No, she didn't seem surprised about the two guys and if her sister told her that much, I wonder why her sister didn't tell her about those flash drives?" I was thinking out loud.

"She said they went to an attorney for those wills and her sister instructed the attorney to mail the envelope she left with him if anything happened to her," Jiff said. "I wonder how we'd ever find out what law firm they went to? There's a ton of attorneys here judging by the number who have ads on billboards all along I-10 and Highway 98."

Jiff and I went back to the boat to see if Daniel needed any help casting off. "Too bad I'm leaving. I wouldn't mind sticking around to help keep an eye on that one," Daniel said nodding up the pier toward the direction Ashley left in. "She's hot, and she sure went to a lot of trouble to find us to make sure Rascal gets to a good home."

"Well, I have her number if your plans change," I said and winked at him.

"Man, if her sister got here Thursday, it sounds like those two were busy over the last day or so," Daniel said coiling one of the lines on the pier.

I nodded in agreement thinking the same thing.

What Daniel said was one more thing added to what was already niggling at me. The way this woman acted wasn't adding up. It seemed the two sisters fast tracked a boatload of changes in her last day. It was only one day they did it all in—the day after she arrived from New York. We found her dead yesterday, so that meant all these changes happened on Friday, the first day she was here. That was after a long, two-day drive from New York to the Florida panhandle. If what Ashley said was true, her sister arrived on Thursday. She was killed on Saturday morning.

Daniel might be on to something with this gal who surrendered Rascal to me. She seemed to know a lot about Rascal, rescue, and microchips, a lot more than someone who doesn't have a pet and just got added on the registration. I started to worry about Rascal being left alone in the condo.

Jiff looked at me and must have been thinking the same thing because he said, "We need to get that dog back to New Orleans… the quicker the better. Those goons will keep looking for him while we're here. Some good Samaritan might see us walking Rascal and tell them where to find us thinking they are doing a good deed."

"Guys?" Daniel said. "I'm already past my departure time."

We hugged, helped him untie lines as he got underway, and waved goodbye.

Chapter Seven

JIFF WAS DRIVING faster than usual and watching the rearview mirror a lot.

"Did I make you paranoid suggesting someone might follow Ashley?"

"I was already paranoid when she showed up," he said. "How do we know she isn't working with them?"

"That didn't occur to me. She seemed genuinely upset over the sister's death and said all the right things to try to get the dog to a safe place," I said. "But one thing is bothering me, well more than one really."

"What?"

"She said the sister came here two days ago with the dog and she didn't want to give us her address because the sister's ex might come looking for her? I'm sure he will come looking for her if he hasn't already, unless he's just glad she's gone. He might want that dog back even if it's not legally his. He lived with it for three years, you know how that is, even bad guys get attached to a dog."

"I think it's time to call our Beach Patrol pal and get him to meet us at the condo," Jiff said. "You have his number?"

"Yes, but I wanted to look at the files first and we won't be able to do that until we get back to New Orleans and our computers," I said.

"There're some computers downstairs in the concierge office they might let us use, if I ask real nice. They should be open by now. I'll see if they'll let us login there for a few minutes," Jiff said.

"That will give me enough time to copy the files and email them to both of us," I said.

"That's what's worrying me. With that guy's name, from Brooklyn, and he has goons down here already, along with hidden flash drives full of some kind of data, I think it could be related to some sort of racketeering, tax evasion or some other criminal activity," Jiff said and his face was set. "The comment she said about her sister finding him with young girls could mean he's involved with human trafficking. None of these are anything we need to get involved in so let's call the Beach Patrol guy Daniel said was working some undercover deal here and let them have it."

"There are a lot of Italians in New York. There's a lot in New Orleans for that matter. It doesn't mean…"

Jiff cut me off. "That's exactly what those flash drives mean."

"We don't know if the ex-husband even knew she had the flash drives. He kicked her out with no money and no worldly possessions. Maybe those are recipes on the drives. She had them hidden in the dog's collar and could have made those copies long before he wanted a divorce. We have a civic duty to know we should hand them over or if we are wasting law enforcement's time."

"You have a point. As much as I would like to give those drives to the authorities and wish I had never seen them, let's take a look at what's on them and then we can make a better decision of what to do," Jiff said.

"I want to check on Rascal first. Ashley has me concerned at what length that ex-husband will go to," I said.

"Ok, let's get him, take him outside and then go see what's on those drives."

All the way to the Penthouse I was worried someone got in and kidnapped Rascal, but he greeted us at the door, tail wagging and spinning in circles enthusiastically. I found a beach towel, wrapped him in it and we went down the service elevator, covertly, to walk him around the grounds. We found a patch of grass somewhat obscure from the road in the parking lot alongside the condo tower. I let Rascal down on the ground using his leash made from sail ties.

"I'll get you a proper leash here soon, boy," I said to him.

After he sniffed around and did what I thought he needed to do, he started to be more interested in playing with us. I wrapped him back up in the towel and took him up to the Penthouse.

Jiff tried to schmooze his way past the front desk clerk who had the worst comb over or wrap around I had ever seen. When we walked up to him, his head was bent down looking at something behind the counter so the top of his head was facing us. His hair was coiled around the top point of his head the way Daniel had coiled the boat lines on the pier. It made the top of his head look like a bull's eye. He didn't look up even though our presence had to cast somewhat of a shadow in his direction.

Finally, Jiff said, "Excuse me." It also didn't seem to impress Comb Over once he noticed us even after Jiff introduced himself and his penthouse condo number. He was clearly annoyed at having been interrupted from whatever it was that had his undivided attention. I looked over the counter and saw it was a crossword puzzle in the local paper.

He replied without a smile or even the attempt at an apology, "It just isn't allowed for anyone to come behind the registration desk." He started to look back to his crossword puzzle when a lady walked up to the counter from a back office. She recognized Jiff as the resident of the Penthouse. After a polite greeting, she walked over to where she raised the counter, allowed us to come through, and invited us back to use the computers in the rear office, her office, "for as long as we liked."

Comb Over offered a stiff smile which caused his eyes to squint but didn't even turn up the farthest corners of his mouth. Then, she said loud enough for him to hear that her name was Victoria and to ask for her if we needed anything else.

Jiff was a lot more adept at finding his way around the drives than I was so he took the lead. The first thing he did was send the files to ourselves in emails. Then he just had to go into his email and start scrolling through them.

"I'm amazed these aren't encrypted," he said.

"If this is a mob thing, are they that sophisticated? Or maybe she copied them for insurance or leverage long before he decided to divorce her," I said. "A lot of men make a big mistake by underestimating how smart a woman really is. We can get a lot of mileage out of blonde hair by acting ditzy. Most men are all too quick to believe it," I said. "Maybe, Abby decided to put her own insurance plan in place and got the dirt on him before he brought up the divorce. She may have made copies of that info even before she married him."

"Sometimes you scare me with the way you think," Jiff said and looked at me.

I just shook my head and rolled my eyes.

Jiff was concentrating on the screen at the first file to open there. It looked like a ledger sheet or computer spread sheet. Whoever managed this business, kept records on a computer. It showed columns of odd words. The only one that I was sure of was DATE. There was one with a list of initials maybe or parts of a name, like three or four letters of a first name and three or four letters of a last name.

My name, Brandy Alexander, would look like branalex if it was on there. There was a column with no heading but initials and a number in each row. Finally, the dates added were in no chronological order and all the dates were in the past. The last column used letters and numbers opposite the previous column that had numbers, then initials. The final column had codes that were all different, BSLG112 or GPM211 or PCBMT121.

Lines looked like this:

```
DATE
2/26/16    BrowManu    10 /MP    DHM108
12/15/15   GalvAnth    25/MP     BSLG112
3/3/17     GartLarr    20/VM     GPM211
```

"This all must mean something incriminating to old Donnato or whoever maintains this spreadsheet," Jiff said. "Unless you know the code, it's going to be meaningless."

"Wait." I printed out what looked like the most current pages yet all the dates were at least a year old. "This looks like old business."

"Now that we've satisfied our curiosity and, in all likelihood, managed to put ourselves in the crosshairs of a major mob hit, let's give this to Mike, our resident beach bum, undercover, Special Forces guy, whoever he is," Jiff said shutting down the file, clearing the history and was about to turn off the computer. "Call him."

"Wait. Before I do that, I want to do one thing." I looked up Abigale Westlake on Facebook. Abigale was a pretty girl, thin, and attractive with long dark hair.

There were several pictures of her with Rascal, with friends at a beach that looked like a Florida beach with pristine white sand, and some on what I assumed was the New Jersey shore. She held up a Stone Pony coaster with a few friends in one photo so I guessed it was New Jersey.

It sure looked like Abby was a party girl from all the bar photos taken and posted with friends. There was another post of her having drinks at a Tiki Bar and one riding next to a big hunky guy in a convertible along a beach that clearly was not in New Jersey. The resemblance to the woman who died on the beach and the woman we met on the pier was striking.

"I want to see one more thing," I said. Then I looked up Ashley Westlake on Facebook. Her Facebook posts looked more professional, standing with models wearing her designs or with an arm around a client who looked stunning in the outfits they were both wearing. They could have been twins they looked so much alike. I showed the screen to Jiff.

"Is that the woman we met this morning?" he asked. Then I showed him the Facebook page for Abby and he said, "It's hard to tell them apart from photos. I wonder if it was easier if you saw them side by side."

"That's why we are going to the Tiki bar in these photos and ask around about her. That guy in the photo looks like he was a good friend or a boyfriend," I said still flipping through the Facebook photos. "He was wearing a T-shirt with the name of a bar on it in

Destin. Let's go there."

"I guess you're thinking what I'm thinking," he said.

"Do we tell Mike?" I asked. "It might get her killed."

"I think not telling Mike might get her killed. She can't pass as her sister with work colleagues, but she could live in her house. If she doesn't have a job, that won't last long," Jiff said.

"If we do figure out she was trying to pass as her sister, it won't be long before her ex-husband figures it out or the FBI, and goes looking for her," I said.

"Maybe they need to find her and ask if she knows what these codes mean on these flash drives," Jiff said. "It might save her. Call Mike."

"I'll call him, but I think he needs to figure it out. He's not gonna want us sticking our nose in it," I said.

🐕 🐕 🐕 🐕 🐕 🐕 🐕 🐕 🐕 🐕

JUST THEN A Security Guard walked by as we left the Concierge Office and stopped when he spotted Jiff.

"Mr. Heinkel, I'm glad I ran into you," he said.

"Hello Wallace. This is my girlfriend, Brandy Alexander," Jiff said by way of introducing us.

I smiled.

"Nice to meet you, Ma'am," Wallace said and nodded his head.

He was holding his security uniform hat under his arm, and his hair was so short I can only describe it as military issue. I guessed him to be early thirties.

"Same here," I said.

"Mr. Heinkel, two men came by here this morning saying they are friends of yours and you were holding their dog for them," Wallace said. "They wanted me to let them into your unit. I told them to contact you and set up a time to meet you here or elsewhere. They left, and they were not happy, but if they stayed around, I was going to call the police. These guys didn't look like anyone you or this lady would socialize with."

"They're not and we think they might have had something to do with the murdered woman," Jiff said.

"I see," said Wallace. "Don't worry about a thing. I'll take care of it if they come around again."

"Wallace is with the Military Police at Hurlburt Field. That's the Air Force Base we pass on our way to Ft. Walton and Destin," Jiff said. "We're lucky to have him here. How's the wife and kids?"

"Family's great, sir. We are expecting our third in a couple of weeks, Thanks for asking," Wallace replied.

"Congratulations and thank you for your service," I said to him.

Wallace smiled, said "Ma'am," and went about his patrol.

Before Jiff could say it, I started dialing my cell, "Okay, I'm calling Mike right now."

Chapter Eight

MIKE RANG THE bell. When I opened the door he was wearing a black suit, button-down shirt with a tie and wingtip shoes. He had on the standard issue of the aviator type sunglasses my imagination had all special forces or special agents wear.

"Special Agent Mike Perricone," he said.

"We met Sunday morning… at the beach… we found the dead girl… remember?" I asked.

He walked right past me and went over to Jiff to shake his hand.

"Wow, you go from the surfboard to the Board Room with such ease," I said. "Don't mind me, I just get the door."

"Funny girl. This is not funny business," he said in a flat tone.

"I see. You change clothes, you change persona. I guess you left the magic personality with your dune buggy and jams."

He ignored me.

After Jiff picked up on how rude I thought Mike was acting, he schmoozed him a bit and mentioned how we all have a mutual friend, Daniel.

Special Agent Mike Perricone said we could call him Mike since we were all friends with Daniel.

Did he want us to think, Oh boy! How cool is that! We get to call the Special Agent by his first name! Who does this dude think he is? He was too impressed with himself.

I also refrained from mentioning that we found the dead body, the dog and the flash drives, not him.

Jiff must have picked up on my body language since I was mentally winding up like a baseball pitcher to throw the drives at Mike's pinhead. He said, "You should thank Brandy. She found those drives sewn inside the dog's collar. They might have gone unnoticed for quite some time if someone else found him or if he lost that collar."

"Really?" was all Mike, who now lacked any magic, could muster.

"Yes, she has worked with homicide in New Orleans as a consultant on several cases," he added. "She really knows this breed since she does rescue for them specifically. We both have Schnauzers as pets."

Okay, Jiff, I think you're laying it on a little heavy, but I was glad to hear him bragging on me to Mr. Special Agent, Moron Mike.

"How exactly does she consult?" he asked Jiff.

"I'm right here so you can ask me," I said and stepped a little closer to him. "I consult because I see things or patterns others miss. I only get involved when, like this murder or situation, I started out as a witness to the crime or if I come across pertinent information that the police miss or did not find. Like the body, the missing dog and the flash drives. I might even see a pattern to what's on those drives since we now met and spoke to the sister of the victim."

"Well, you won't be working as a consultant with my unit or any kind of consultant, Miss Dog Lady."

By now, Jiff had picked up the drives to hand them to Mike. I was moving from mentally aiming at his head to actually throwing them at his head.

"The data on those drives are on a need to know basis, so we won't need to consult you on that either. What did the sister want from you?" Mike asked.

"She didn't want anything from us," I said.

"What did you tell her?" he asked and took a step closer to me.

"That's on a need to know basis," I said and walked over to the door.

"She asked if she could surrender the dog to Brandy and she did," Jiff answered. He played much better in this sandbox.

"We have a signed document allowing her to do that, and she had a legal document giving her that right. Then she left," I said to him.

"I'm curious how she knew where to find us?" Jiff said.

"She mention the drives?" Mike asked ignoring Jiff's question moving into my personal space.

I took a tiny step closer to him, waited until I saw him blink, waited a few more seconds, and then asked, "Why would she? It was her sister's dog."

He took a small step back.

I turned, walked to the door, opened it wide, and said, "Thanks for coming to pick these up." As soon as I didn't think I'd actually hit him closing the door, I let it slam.

Jiff just looked at me. "It might not be a good idea to alienate him."

"We did him a favor, several actually, so he should be worrying about alienating us. He's rude."

"He didn't answer either of us when we asked how Ashley knew how to find us. Those two guys knew the dog was with Daniel and they could have seen us. I don't think those goons were doing any Good Samaritan work, like finding the dog to return to the owner. I think they were looking for the dog to return to Abby's ex-husband," I said and put both hands on top my head interlocking my fingers.

"Now what do you want to do?" he asked me smiling.

"I think we need a distraction and something to take our mind off this for a while," I said and wrapped my arms around his waist. "I want to go swimming, and this evening, I want to go to that Tiki Bar."

🐕 🐕 🐕 🐕 🐕 🐕 🐕 🐕 🐕 🐕

JIFF AND I headed to Destin, home of the Tiki hut bar

advertised on the shirt the guy in the Facebook picture was wearing with Ashley in the convertible. Our plan was to enjoy the sunset view and to covertly wait and see if the two guys who beat up Daniel showed up. Not a great plan, I must admit. We had absolutely no expectation for success, but we could enjoy a drink or two and sit with a waterfront view while we watched the world go by.

I hoped doing something that was far from the Daniel, Ashley, Rascal, and the dead woman would allow my separate thoughts flow around and find another thought to associate with.

We found seats at the big square bar that sat in the middle of all things Tiki, officially known as Big Al's World Famous Tiki Hut Bar and Restaurant. It overlooked the Gulf of Mexico in Destin. That was all on the sign that took up the entire front of the building. Who knew Destin had anything world famous, let alone someone named Big Al and his Tiki bar?

I loved the place immediately even if it hadn't been world famous. It was my kind of beach bar. It was an open-air bar with several tables both bar height and dining height, a stage for a band, dance floor and a gift shop. The entire place, bar area, restaurant, dance floor, and stage, was covered in a giant—you guessed it—a big Tiki hut roof. The bar was a short ride from any boat slip to open water. Of course, open water was right at the Tiki Hut's back door. The bar and restaurant looked to be about thirty steps up from the pier level where all the boats docked.

"Boy, this place is great," Jiff said, "even if we are on a quasi-stakeout."

Every size and type of watercraft was going in and out of the marina. It was non-stop entertainment with every kind of boat one could imagine and then some.

A big yellow boat painted like a banana on each side came into view from the Gulf and started to put-put in the no wake zone heading to a slip which was right down in front of Big Al's. The slip had a wooden archway and header on it that read, RIDE BIG AL'S WORLD FAMOUS BANANA BOAT!

I was starting to see a trend here and I would have bet the farm that the owner of the world-famous bar also owned the world-famous banana boat. When it finally docked, and the lines held it secure in the slip, a deckhand opened the gangplanks for the visitors to exit. About fifty people with various stages of sunburn, spilled off and came right up the stairs to the Tiki Hut.

"The boat parade in and out of this harbor was non-stop. The marina is way bigger than it looks," I said and Jiff nodded his agreement.

"Like that Banana Boat, objects are closer than they appear," Jiff teased.

We ordered a wine for me and beer for Jiff and settled into our two places at the bar. The nosiness of the other bar patrons checking us out had worn off by the time our drinks arrived. I showed the Facebook photo of Abigale in the convertible to the bartender asking, "Do you know this gal? Is this the girl who was in the paper this morning?"

She shook her head no, but in a lowered voice as she leaned across the bar to place a cocktail napkin under each drink and said, "Yep. That was her sister's photo in the paper this morning. Ashley Westlake was murdered on the beach yesterday."

The bartender moved non-stop, poured several beers from the different taps, filled a waiter's tray, rang it up on a register. She waived over the waiter whose order she filled. He walked by, left two twenty-dollar bills and she rang it up and left the change on his tray. He picked it up without checking anything on his way back past the bar.

This was multi-tasking at its best. She looked busy, and it didn't look like she had much time for chit chatting.

"I thought the paper said her name was Abigale Westlake," I said when she came back to us to see if we needed another round. I had a confused look on my face.

She took her time finding the right bottle of wine to refill my glass and refill Jiff's beer while she said to us, "She had a sister named Abigail. I knew them both. Ashley came back here after school. Abby stayed in New York. They went to school together for fashion design," she said watching the door from the parking lot. She waved over a waiter and said, "These two people would like a table on the rail to watch the sunset. I'll move their tab with them."

I realized she meant us when he picked up our drinks and put them on his tray and said, "Follow me." She gave me a wide-eyed look that suggested I follow the waiter. When the waiter left with our drinks in the direction she nodded, she leaned over the bar to wipe our area clean saying to me, "I'll be right over to take your order."

As Jiff followed the waiter to the table, I bent down to pick up my purse from the floor. When I stood up, two men were waiting for me to leave so they could claim our seats at the bar. One of them had a large homemade or prison tattoo in the shape of an upside-down U on his forearm. They climbed in the seats as I turned my back away from them.

I waved at Jiff when he looked around I gave him the signal I used to tell him I'm going to the ladies' room. I make a motion like I'm putting on invisible lipstick. He nodded that he saw me. Instead, I went to the world-famous gift shop just inside the entrance. I bought each of us a straw, fedora-style hat and the ugliest beach shirt for Jiff I knew he would never buy for himself.

Those guys didn't recognize me from the night they beat up Daniel, but I thought they might recognize Jiff. He always looked polished and neat, even in topsiders. The hat and shirt would make him blend in with the people who were pouring off the Banana Boat downstairs. He needed a sunburn to make his cover one hundred percent. Now we would look like every other couple in the place.

I hurried back to the table and gave him what I bought saying, "Put this on. I think that's the two guys from the pier incident who just came in and took our seats at the bar. I got you a shirt you can put on over the one you're wearing. You'll look a little Magnum PI with the hat and Hawaiian shirt, like all the other tourists in here. Keep your sunglasses on and move to that chair." I nodded to the chair with his back to the bar.

At the table I took the seat that faced the door, the bar, and looked into the marina. The Gulf of Mexico was at my back. I made Jiff move, so he faced the Gulf with his back to where the two guys were sitting. I could keep an eye on them without looking like I was watching them.

We started to look at the menus the waiter left with us. Jiff thought we might need something to munch on. We needed to compensate for the multiple drinks we might be having in order to get some face time with the bartender to ask more questions.

The band meandered in and began setting up and doing some sound tests. The bartender came over with two more drinks for us and put them on our table. She had a pad and pen with her like she was going to take our order.

"If either of those guys look around over here, let

me know and I'll have to leave," she said. "You two look like the nice couple that found Ashley on the beach."

"We are, but how would you know that?" Jiff asked.

"The paper said a nice couple and my sister is the woman cop that took your information at the scene. She described you both, said you're a private detective from New Orleans and this guy is a criminal attorney and your boyfriend. You're kinda hard to miss," she said and made a face at Jiff. Since I hadn't seen her smile at anyone, I guessed this was the closest she came to getting friendly.

"Wow, small world here and news travels fast," Jiff said.

"You have no idea," our bartender, now our waitress, said.

"We think those two guys jumped our friend the other night," I nodded to the two at the bar. "Our friend Daniel found Rascal, and those gumballs tried to take your friend, the dead girl's dog," I said. I kept my sunglasses on in case those guys turned around.

"Rascal was Abby's dog. I don't know why Ashley would have been walking him unless Abby asked her to. Abby took advantage of Ashley every chance she got, and Ashley let her."

"Did you know Abby just got back here on Thursday and was staying with Ashley?" I asked.

"No, but it doesn't surprise me. Abby always had

problems, and she called Ashley to listen to them or bail her out. Those two guys are the type of problems that Abby always had," she said and started to wipe off our table and clear the empty glasses.

"Have you seen them before?" I asked.

"They came in here late last night. They started drinking shots. A lot of shots. I've been doing this long enough to know those two scare me and I don't want anything to do with them. I especially don't want to cross them. Last night they asked me where the Destin marina was. I told them you're sitting in it. They're idiots," she said putting cocktail napkins, then setting our drinks down.

"But, I get the impression they are very mean idiots," I said.

"The one with the long hair kept playing with a plastic marker. It looked like it had a combination code to a locker on it," she said.

"Did you see what it was to?" Jiff asked her tapping his finger on the table like he was trying to make up his mind.

"They sat at the bar and drank shots. The short one ragged on him to put it back in his pocket. I found it under the money they paid when they left. They were both too drunk to know they dropped it when they stumbled out of here," she said. It was a key on a round plastic ring like airport lockers use. It said DHM108. It looked like a key to a storage locker. "Just now I gave it back to them and said someone found it on the bar after they left. It was in the lost and found drawer behind the bar."

"Why are you telling us this?" Jiff asked.

"Telling you what?" She started jotting some things down on the pad on the tray. "The grilled fish fingers are Grouper, a good choice."

"There are cameras all over this place," she said writing on her menu pad. "I don't want anyone thinking I found something I shouldn't have found and kept it. Not good for anyone's longevity."

"They've ordered those shots and asked me if I was working last night. They can't even remember who served them. I said I was here working tables," she said, head down, writing. When she looked up, she tapped on the menu in Jiff's hand like she was referring to something. "Beverly Frederick is the lady cop you met. She liked you and you should give anything you find to her, and not that idiot, who thinks he's fooling everyone with that Beach Patrol disguise. He'll take it and any credit for whatever it leads to. If you find something, loop Beverly in is all I ask."

"My name is Brandy, and this is Jiff," I said.

"Forgive me if I don't shake. I don't' want anyone thinking I know you. I'm your server, Jess," she nodded and wrote something down on her order pad. "I'm ordering you two a couple of appetizers, on me," she said softly and then in a normal voice, she added, "That will be right out." She left to turn in whatever she ordered for us and went back to the bar.

"Well, what do you make of that?" Jiff asked leaning into me and holding my hand.

"Maybe she wants a big tip," I said smiling at him. "I think she really knows more than what she's telling us. This is a small community, and it's the off season. Everyone seems to know or see what goes on here," I said. "If they don't, they know someone who does."

"Like home."

"I think this place is a lot smaller and more 'in your business' than what we're used to in New Orleans," I said. "If Jess gives this info to her friend, I could see how Magic Mike would bulldoze her and take credit."

"Or maybe it would bring a lot of attention to Jess working here at the World Famous Tiki Bar. She probably can't afford to lose her job," Jiff said. He polished off his second beer. "When she brings our food, let's get another round. It might keep her coming back with more info."

"If it's known she's conspiring with or snitching to the police, it might get the attention of someone here. I'm not saying it about this one, but bars are notorious for being involved in shady stuff. They don't want to bring the cops around unnecessarily," I said.

"Well, we need to hear what else this gal can tell us before we split," he started waving at Jess for another round.

"Slow down there, cowboy. I don't want to carry you home. She'll be back when our food is ready. We don't want to rush her," I said taking the hand he had raised and kissing it.

"Didn't you say that Abby was in the car with someone wearing a shirt advertising this place? Maybe he works here. Let's ask Jess when she brings our food," Jiff said.

We waited for our order and enjoyed the sunset while sunburned people from the Banana Boat made their way up the stairs from the pier. They filled up every vacant table and started a wait list with the hostess near the gift shop entrance. I could see Jess working like a fiend at the bar. The two goons were ordering shots and slamming them back.

A burly guy with a bald head, tattoos from his neck to his wrists on both arms, and his wallet chained to his belt loop came from somewhere behind the stage. He took over making drinks. Jess picked up her order pad and went to check on orders in the kitchen. I saw the big bald-headed guy shake his head to the two raising their hands for another round.

A second big muscular guy with a mullet haircut and wearing a T-shirt that looked spray painted on him with the world-famous logo and SECURITY in large letters across the back came from behind the stage. He stood behind the two at the bar. When the burly bartender gave them their change, they stood up with an attitude until they realized they were a head shorter than both of the Tiki workers. The Tiki security guy escorted them out to the parking lot.

"I think there is an office with security monitors

behind that stage," I said to Jiff after I described what was happening.

"Don't be obvious, but Jess was right. There are cameras all over this place. Check out the overhead beams strung with lights. There's a camera that looks a lot like a light every few feet. I bet Big Al doesn't have much theft here," Jiff said. "I bet it's easy to pull them down with the lights when he has to bug outta here for storms too."

"That's smart of Big Al to put so many cameras in his restaurant. Must be why he's world famous," I said smiling.

With the restaurant and bar packed, Jess didn't get back to our table but one more time. Other waiters were offering to take orders, but we waved them off. She came with our food and another round of drinks. When I asked her about the guy in the car with Ashley on Facebook she said, "That guy owns this place. He was too rough for Ashley.

"That's Abby in that picture she posted on Ashley's page. Abby came down here every two months or so, supposedly to work with Ashley on the fashion business that Ashley did all the design on. Instead, she got a spray tan and hit this place every night without her wedding ring.

"Abby used to date Big Al in high school, back when everyone used to call him Flashpole. That's how I know all of them. He's also chummy with good ole Magic Mike. It's dangerous knowing some of these people. It was for Ashley having a sister like Abby."

"But that's Abby we found on the beach," Jiff started to say.

"Look harder," she said softly. After she finished clearing our table of food, plates and glasses, she added loudly, "Thank you, come again," as she picked up a generous tip Jiff left with the bill.

Chapter Nine

JIFF AND I took a stroll along the pier after paying the check at the Tiki Hut. What Jess said had me mentally going over everything I thought we knew. If cameras were everywhere Jiff, and I had a silent understanding not to speak about anything we just heard in public. We would talk in the car or back at the condo. The smell of fresh fish was stronger on the pier as we walked along. It had occasionally wafted up to our table while we sat in the restaurant. We passed the Banana Boat and watched it being cleaned for the next day's sail. There was a continuous line of party boats bringing in day trippers who had gone out to catch a big one on vacation. Workers were hosing down boats and cleaning fish.

The commercial fleet started right after the party boat slips. The fish smell got stronger. Many were cleaning their daily catch to sell to restaurants or places that sold fresh seafood. As we left the commercial fishing boat end of the pier we walked into and around a parking lot to pick up the marina again. This time the boats looked to be privately owned sailboats and motor yachts. I smelled new fiberglass and canvas. The fish smell was gone unless the wind changed direction.

"Well, check this out," Jiff said stopping in front of a Hatteras all tricked out with every navigational instrument on the fly bridge. It had a new boat shine going on and the name across the stern was Big Al's World Famous Fishing Boat. There were dock boxes all along both sides of the pier behind every boat.

"Does Big Al own anything that's not world famous?" I asked as we both stood there looking at the very big, very expensive hole his boat made in the water.

We continued to walk to the end of the private pier past more power or sailboats both large and small. We stopped at the end to admire the marina in all its calmness.

"How come we've never heard of all this world famous-ness?" I pulled out my cell and Googled 'Big Al, Destin, Florida'. Then I clicked on his website and showed Jiff what scrolled up.

Big Al also seemed to be world famous for a string of fishing charters up and down the gulf coast from Bay St. Louis to Panama City. Then I Googled the Secretary of State in Florida for the owner's complete name.

"Jess said his real name is Al Flashpole. With a name like Flashpole I could see why he went with Big Al," I said.

"Of course, Flashpole might be helpful if he was in

the strip club business," Jiff mused.

"Hang on to that thought," I said. I looked up all businesses owned in Florida by Al Flashpole and Voila! A string of fitness centers and strip clubs popped up along the gulf coast from Mississippi to Florida, in the same cities the fishing charter boats were docked. There was a new one in Slidell, Louisiana, not far from Bay St. Louis and on the water. Bars, boats, strip clubs and gyms. My mind was spinning.

"What are you thinking?" Jiff asked. "I'm wondering how they all connect."

"Yeah, now you're curious too? They connect, but I'm not seeing it yet," I said.

"You know, I think we ought to call Jess's friend, that lady cop, the one we met on the beach. She might be a little more forthcoming with the Abby and Ashley story and have the time to tell us. Jess is clearly afraid to say too much in that place," Jiff said and looked around to see who might be in hearing distance. It seemed like we were all alone. We didn't see anyone on any of the yachts.

"If I had a big boat like one of these, I'd be on it every spare second," he said. Then he added, "With you. What's your favorite type boat?"

"I like all boats, but I love sailboats," I answered him. "I think I could live on a sailboat."

"Big boats like Daniel has?" he asked.

Smiling, I answered him, "Any size or any kind of boat as long as I'm on it… with you."

He pulled me to him and we kissed out at the end of the pier where no one was around but we could be seen from a long way off. It felt very private, but it was anything but. The marina was super-wide at this point and went from a channel to an open area like a cul-de-sac in neighborhoods. This was a huge cul-de-sac for slips and all around the perimeter of the marina were three to eight story condo buildings or apartments. There were many windows from which spying eyes could see us at the end of this pier, no matter how alone we felt.

As we strolled back down the pier heading back to our car, I stopped abruptly.

"What's up?" Jiff turned to see why I was standing still.

"Look at what's stenciled on Big Al's dock box and on the pier behind his boat," I said pretending to rummage in my purse. I pulled out a tissue.

"Yeah, it's DMH108. Why does that number look like we've seen it somewhere before?"

"We have, and very recently," I said and pretended to blow my nose. It felt like an icy cold finger running down my back.

DMH108 was painted on three sides of the dock box. You couldn't miss it. There was one on the walkway side, and one on each side facing up and down the pier. The box was made up of two separate sides, one large one with a combo lock and a smaller side that could hold a gym or duffle bag with a key lock. When I looked around at the other dock boxes, some just had numbers or no markings whatsoever. Each boat slip had a number stenciled in yellow paint on the concrete pier. They all started with DMH for Destin Marina Harbor with the number of the slip each boat was docked in.

"Jiff, in case someone is watching let's look like lovers. Kiss me and look over my shoulder at that number on Big Al's dock box," I barely whispered to him.

Jiff was quick to accommodate my request by nibbling my ear and saying, "I know where we've seen it. It's on one of those flash drives."

"Yes. Don't say anything else until we get to the car. Let's just keep walking and stopping a little on our way back. Anyone could be watching us out here."

We strolled back down that pier hand in hand to the car.

Going over in my head, I wondered *what do we really know?* We found a dead woman who we think lost her dog. We went on a sailing cruise where we found the dog and then the muggers tried to take him. The sister found us—the living sister of the dead person doesn't want the dog but surrenders him to rescue. We now know the number on Big Al's dock box matches a number on that flash drive. It's the same number on a key the two at the bar reclaimed according to Jess.

"I'm having trouble seeing how it all adds up, but I

know it does, don't you?" I asked Jiff once we were in the car.

Jiff was sitting behind the wheel with his arms crossed. He bumped his fist on his chin. This was his processing mode. His eyes were moving around and I waited until he was ready to deliver some output. The chin bumping accelerated.

"I got nothing," he finally said.

"Let's go back to the condo. I'm sure Rascal needs to take a walk by now."

"Tomorrow, I think we need to talk to that lady cop you made friends with," he said. "After we walk Rascal, I'm taking you for a romantic stroll on the beach."

OUR ROMANTIC STROLL on the beach was a rehash of what we knew. Jiff brought it up. I'm usually the one who can't let go of the puzzle until I find an answer. He's just as bad since, as a criminal attorney, he has to try to figure out who else might have done it if he wants to get his client off the hook. It was refreshing to work with someone like him to try to figure it out. He always respected my input and even if he disagreed with me, he explained why and sometimes he changed his mind back to my way of thinking.

"So, let's think about what we know or think we know," he said. "We find a girl dead on the beach, with a dog leash around her wrist and the leash lets us know the dog's name is Rascal. We find the dog, coincidentally, with the name Rascal on the collar that matches the leash the same evening we take a sunset sail and I know the owner of the boat. Daniel is jumped by the same two at the bar. They were trying to take the dog. Then you find those flash drives. One of the entries on the flash drive matches a boat slip number to some local businessman here."

"Yes. I'm glad we found Rascal. But what's bothering me is the course of events after we found him. If we had been five minutes late, those two guys who mugged Daniel would have taken him," I said.

Jiff added, "How did they find Rascal at that boat? His owner was killed at least twenty miles from that marina even if he did say he went into Fort Walton or Destin to pick up parts."

"How did those two guys come to your condo in your building knowing we had Rascal? Who knew we had him? The couple on the boat who helped us, Daniel, you, me. The police? Harbormaster?" I asked out loud. I had more questions than either of us had answers.

"If the gal we met this morning is Abby and not Ashley, why didn't she want her dog back or at least to see him and make sure he wasn't hurt? The fact that she didn't—if it was her dog—is kinda bothering me, but I'm just glad he's with us in a safe place. If it really was Ashley, why didn't she want to see her sister's dog to make sure he was not harmed, and why didn't she want to keep him? It seems like the sort of thing you would do for your sister who was murdered—take care of her pet as a connection."

"Yeah, I'd want to see Isabella one last time. I'd have to confirm she was not hurt if I was letting her go to another home, or if someone close to me was killed and she was their dog. We've not paid attention to the dead girl or why someone wanted her dead. The sister who found us, and how did she do that by the way? She told us the ex-husband in New York did it. She didn't mention the flash drives and didn't really ask us anything. She wanted to surrender the dog to us, officially," I said.

"She wanted us to think it's the ex-husband who did it? She implied the ruthless ex-husband who left Abby penniless could be connected," Jiff said putting air quotes around connected.

"You know what I'm wondering? What if the one we met this morning is Abby, the one from New York who owns the dog and she wants us to believe she is the dead sister, Ashley? Could this be her own version of witness protection?"

"Well, yes, that might explain some of it, but not all. I say we get her investigated. I'll call my office tomorrow and get one of the researchers on it," Jiff said pulling me close to him as the waves licked at our ankles.

"We could use Facebook to see what preliminary information we can find and if we hit a snag, then you can make the call. Although it would be easier on a laptop instead of my iPhone."

"I thought you might say that so I sent a text to Tom, my assistant. I asked him to have my personal laptop couriered over here tomorrow morning unless he finds a way to get it here sooner," Jiff said.

I threw my arms around his neck and gave him a big hug.

"We make a good team don't you think?" he said.

"I think we do. Now, let's enjoy this moonlight walk on the beach while we wait on that laptop," I said. I pulled Jiff's arm around my neck and shoulders leaning into him under his arm as we walked in the wet sand along the water's edge.

Chapter Ten

"ARE YOU AWAKE?" Jiff asked me. We were both still in bed, staying very still as to not wake the other.

"No, I'm sound asleep," I answered him. "I'm surprised you're awake."

It was six-thirty a.m., and we had a long day yesterday. Rascal was sleeping in the king-size bed with us. He was on my side, above my head, on my pillow, against the headboard, like I was sleeping with a hat on.

"Well, wake up, Blondie," Jiff teased calling me a name he knew made me crazy. He rolled over on his side to face me lying on my back staring at the ceiling. "Because this is our last day here unless we extend our stay a day, which I can do." He tweaked my nose as he got out of bed. "C'mon, you're usually on Marine Time, not me."

"Marine Time?"

"Marines get more done by eight a.m., than most people do all day. It could be your motto 'cuz I don't want to see you joining the Marines. Their mandatory haircut would not look good on you."

"It's Monday. I'll call and extend my time off by a day or two. I have meetings at the end of the week I have to be back for," I said rolling out of bed but letting Rascal sleep in. "I know this is not the relaxing trip you wanted for us."

"I don't know. I need my mind sharp to keep up with you. Besides, this is more exciting than lying around worrying about getting sunburned," he said. "Did you see those people who got off the Banana Boat?"

That made me laugh.

"Call that lady cop and I'll check with Tom and see when to expect my laptop," Jiff said throwing on a pair of shorts.

He rummaged through the closet for a shirt and then decided a polo was a better idea. Jiff had a swimmer's body, tall, lean but muscular in all the right places. He had a six pack for a stomach and was never impressed with his own good looks. His down-to-earth personality was refreshing and a reflection of the way he was raised. His parents were wealthy, and adopted all of their six children, Jiff was the oldest. They were so kind and generous you wished you could clone them to be everyone's parents, particularly your own.

"Let's go lay by the pool or walk on the beach for a while. It's early and I doubt the officer will be in yet and I bet that computer doesn't arrive before nine o'clock. Besides, I want to see you without a shirt for a little while longer," I said.

The morning walk on the beach was rife with shells. They were rolling in with the waves. I'd spot a beautiful shell and would grab it before the outgoing wave would pull it away. There were tons of shells beached from the previous tide coming in and depositing them along the sand where I could see them. I could not stop myself from picking one up every few steps and checking out its beauty.

"You're like my mother," Jiff said.

This was a huge relief that he didn't say I was like *my* mother. "How so?" "She can't stop herself from picking up shells and seeing if they deem worthy of saving. The thing is, she deems all the ones she picks up worthy of saving. That's why every container in our condo is overflowing with shells. Didn't you notice? If you start opening cabinets you will find jars, bags, containers of shells in all of them. My Dad said if she keeps collecting them we might have to leave the condo to the shells and move out here on the beach. I brought you something," he said and pulled a plastic bag you get at a grocery from the back pocket of his shorts. "I knew you'd pick them up and now you have a place to put them."

Jiff constantly surprised me with his thoughtfulness. "Thanks," I said and put the shell in the plastic grocery bag he was holding out. "See, now your Mom and I have something in common."

"When I was a kid, she told me she had been fascinated by shells her entire life. Now, I must tell you, my mother also says you'll be a slave to collecting once you pick up the first one and save it. She says she just can't stop herself." He took the bag from me and held it up. "I'll hold the bag so you can use two hands to search."

I had already bent my knees and was searching a mound of shells with both hands. I found a fascinating white shell that I once heard called a Baby's Ear. It was a soft white on white and had circling bands of soft white did look like a baby's ear.

We stayed on the beach while I looked for shells and Jiff held the plastic collection bag for me to put my finds in. I'd see him pull out one I just put in the bag to observe more closely. Sometimes he would just say "Hmm," or he might offer the name of the shell. We, correction, I looked for shells for about an hour and a half, while Jiff followed along beside me. He never complained. Sometimes he'd point out one that he thought looked interesting. I always picked it up and put it in the bag. When he suggested we head in to call the lady cop and check for deliveries, I couldn't believe we'd been out here so long.

"I guess I like this a lot more than I imagined," I said. I couldn't help myself from stopping to pick up something that looked interesting as we made our way across the sand back to the walkway over the dunes. "You seem to know the names of more shells than I do. Perhaps, you're a little more into shelling than you care to admit."

"I couldn't help learning the names when I was a

kid. My mom would clean them, line them all up to dry and then tell us names of the ones she knew. I liked doing it with her. My brothers didn't and my sister was just a baby," he said.

Jiff started to clean the shells I collected while I went and took my shower.

BY THE TIME we showered and dressed it was almost nine o'clock. My job was to continue to take the shells out of the cleaning solution and place them on paper towels to dry. Jiff was in the shower when I heard a knock on the door. It was Jiff's assistant who drove over from New Orleans with his laptop. Boy, I needed an assistant like Tom. He unboxed it, plugged it in and had it booting up when Jiff came out dressed.

"Mr. Heinkel, I couldn't find a courier that would get your computer here this early and I was afraid they might damage it. I drove it over and brought your printer if you want that too?" Tom said when he saw Jiff.

"I know I would benefit from seeing some of this printed out," I said to Jiff. Part of my gift in life was seeing the similarities or discrepancies in things. I worked for a major telecom company in the fraud prevention unit. I found irregular patterns in calling/phone records for companies. I used computers sometimes, but finding something out of place, visually, was my thing. I was good at it. Jiff nodded to

Tom, and he hurried off to bring up the printer and paper he had in the car.

"Tom, thanks for driving this over. We could've waited another hour or so for a courier," Jiff said as he helped him set up the printer and computer.

TOM ACCEPTED A cup of coffee and stayed long enough to make sure everything was working and Jiff didn't need his help with anything further. Then he got ready to drive back to New Orleans.

Rascal came running out to bark at Tom when he finally decided to wake up.

"Jiff, do you think we should send Rascal back with Tom?" I asked him. "Those two guys have tried to take him twice, once from Daniel at his boat, and then from here. Maybe three times if you count the morning of the murder. What if we stay another day and get tied up somewhere? I don't want to leave him all day locked up in here and who can we trust to walk him?"

"That's a good idea. It would be one less thing we'd have to worry about if we have to stay longer," Jiff said.

"Could Tom drop him off at my apartment? Suzanne won't mind. She's watching Meaux and Isabella for us and it's only another day or so."

"Tom, wait up," he said and started collecting all of Rascals stuff. "I've got a passenger for you to ride back with."

"I'll take him anywhere you want, but I can't take him home. If my kids see the dog, they will cry and want to keep him. My wife will kill me. Tell your friend I'll be at your house by three this afternoon," Tom said.

"If she can't be there, we'll text you my groomer's name and address and you can leave him there," I told him.

I made the arrangements and sent Tom the address of the groomer while Jiff helped Tom get all of Rascal's worldly possessions down to the car. The last text I sent was to my groomer asking him to send me a text and let me know the second Tom dropped off Rascal.

I started looking at the files before they came back. There were notations to look at different files and one was referencing a file or transaction that I could not find on any of the four flash drives. There were no files from this week on any of the drives we had copied and given to Mike.

I ran to find my purse and pulled out the sleeve. There were no more files in the sleeve. I went to check Rascal's collar more closely, and there was something tightly sewn in behind the clasp. It was easy to miss if I hadn't taken a second, closer look. When I ripped open the seam another, smaller thumb drive with a plastic removable cover was stitched inside. It was smaller than the other four drives.

"Look what I found," I said when Tom and Jiff returned to take Rascal down.

"Whoever did this planned on the four drives in the sleeve being a distraction in case Rascal was found.

Whoever was looking would probably figure they had found them all."

"Can I take my travelling companion now?" Tom asked.

"Yeah, I think we have everything we need. Be careful Tom and don't stop for anything until you get to NOLA," Jiff said. "Call me if you need anything, and call or text when you get there and drop Rascal, please."

After Tom left, I was antsy to see what was on this drive. I was going to examine it from the beginning to the end before Jiff wanted me to call Mike and hand it over.

"I'm gonna let it rip, potato chip," I said popping in the drive.

And rip it did. The earlier files we found on the previous drives had data on them that was years old and out of date. This one was current, very current with no past dates or any dates entered as if entries needed to be completed. It showed that there was a name on the list of westabig, 500K/ and ending with PCBM999 on that row. There was no DATE in that column.

I imagined Officer B. Frederick was on call by now since she and her partner came out Saturday morning early when we found the body. I called the number she had written down on the note she gave me and I expected to get the police station. Instead, Officer Beverly Frederick answered stating her full name.

After I told her who I was, I asked if she remembered me. She did. I told her I found the dog.

"You might get a call from the sister of the vic. She called here asking if we found the dog. I'm sorry, but my young, new partner was on the desk told her about the mugging at the marina in Pensacola over a Schnauzer. She might try to contact you."

"She showed up at the marina when we brought our friend back to his boat. We didn't find the dog, he did," I said.

"A lady called in a report saying two guys tried to mug a man with a dog at that marina. Is that the same man?"

"Yes, the man who found the dog has a sailboat, a catamaran, more of a sailing yacht actually, out there. We went on a sunset cruise with him. He gave Rascal to me and my boyfriend after he learned that I do rescue," I said. "He had planned to post the dog on Facebook and take him to the shelter if he didn't find the owner."

"Well, good. I'm glad the little guy got to you after all," Officer B. Frederick said.

"We would like to talk to you, Officer Frederick, preferably not at the station. I found something I probably should not have seen, but I did. We turned the ones I found initially over to Mike Perricone yesterday. I found another one, and I think you should come see this. We also met Jess who works at Big Al's Tiki bar and she told us something we think we've made a connection to. Can you come to our condo?" I asked.

"Sure. I can be there is fifteen minutes. Is that Okay?"

"Yes." I said, and she hung up without saying goodbye. Dante used to do this to me and so does Hanky. It must be a cop thing. Nothing annoys me more than when someone does not end the conversation by saying goodbye, or something similar, and just hangs up. Phone etiquette is a thing of the past.

Chapter Eleven

OFFICER FREDERICK SHOWED up on time, in exactly fifteen minutes. After exchanging pleasantries, she got right to the point.

"I don't have much time. I did call your friend, Detective Zide Hanky in New Orleans. She seems nice, and she had a lot of good things to say about the both of you. Hanky said I could trust you with my life, which is more than I can say for one or two of the rookie officers I work with here," she said. "She put her Captain on the line who echoed the same thing and said to give you a wide berth. He said we could trust you to do the right thing."

"Her Captain? Who?" I asked. "Not Captain Deedler?"

"Yes. Deedler, that was his name."

"Captain Dante Deedler?" I asked again and could feel my face scrunch up.

"Yes, him."

That had me flummoxed so as I sat there with a look of disbelieve on my face. Jiff jumped in with "We've both have worked closely with Captain Deedler and Detective Hanky as consultants to help with a case. Brandy and I share a mutual respect for them and we're glad to hear they have the same for us."

"Captain Deedler didn't mention you," she said to Jiff. "Detective Hanky did."

"So, let me show you what we found on that drive," Jiff continued.

"You looked at this?" Officer Frederick asked.

"Yes. We gave the first ones we found to special agent Mike Perricone. He didn't seem impressed."

"He told you he's a special agent? He was with the Bureau but then they wanted to boot him out so my captain gave him a job as an undercover detective in our unit," she said. "He's no special agent, in fact, he's not that good of a detective either. He thinks if he says he still works for the FBI often enough, it will happen again. He's delusional."

Jiff and I looked at each other. "He introduced himself when he came here dressed in a black suit, shirt and tie as Special Agent Mike Perricone," Jiff said. "He didn't say he was with the FBI, we more or less assumed it."

"Of course, you did, because he said he was a special agent and not an undercover lifeguard/detective. The FBI guys called him Baywatch. That's what most of us now call him," she said and laughed.

I almost felt sorry for him but didn't.

Officer Frederick continued, "He was impressed when he got those flash drives and couldn't wait to see what was on them. That data was old news. There wasn't anything on those drives pointing to a current deal or payoff coming up," Frederick said. "There wasn't even one in the recent past we could connect. That's the only reason our unit got to look at them because they were worthless according to our Special Agent Magic Mike." She air quoted special agent. "He will only call us as back up if he thinks he is going to get his butt kicked. He's a glory hound."

"You did see the data on them, right?" I asked.

"Yes."

"Well, what can you tell from it? I'll tell you what I think I know, if you tell me what you know," I said.

"I'm not sure how much I can share with you. I can share this," she said. She handed me the report on Daniel's mugging at the Marina in Pensacola, pier Nine, in slip number 9999. It read where a couple on another boat in slip 901 observed it and was asked to call it in. The victim was going to someone's home to recover. The report said two men were trying to take a dog named Rascal. This couple in slip 901 said they later learned the dog belonged to the woman killed on the beach that morning.

According to Officer Frederick, the new recruit, now on extended probation, had given out information without asking his superiors and was told he may have endangered others.

I updated Officer Frederick about Ashley Westlake waiting on the pier when we arrived. Ashley told us when we got there, a couple directed her to Daniel's boat at the end of the pier. They told her we would be back this morning, pointed to his boat Daniel was on, so she waited near it. The woman introduced herself to us as Ashley Westlake, provided a Power of Attorney giving her the right to act on behalf of her sister, Abigale Westlake. She didn't want the dog back due to her inability to financially care for the dog.

"Really? What did she want from you?"

"All she asked was if we were sure his name was Rascal. I told her it was on his collar, and she said, 'Oh, good, he was still wearing his collar.' She seemed relieved he still had it."

"She never mentioned the drives Brandy found sewn inside the collar. She knew so much about her sister, Abby's business. In one day she managed to get a power of attorney to act on her sister's behalf in case she died, and knew a lot about Rascal when he wasn't even her dog," Jiff said. "Don't you find that odd?"

"Not if you knew Abby Westlake. We all went to the same high school. Jess, the bartender you met working at Big Al's Tiki Hut, was in Ashley's class and I was a year ahead of them. Abby ran with a fast crowd. She was always on the brink of trouble," Officer Frederick said. "What made you go to the Tiki Bar Big Al owns? Was it curious tourist-type interest or something in particular made you go there?"

"While I do love a good beach front bar, I looked on their Facebook pages and saw one of them in a convertible with a guy wearing a Big Al's T-shirt," I said.

"Brandy happened to show Jess that Facebook photo and ask her about it instead of someone else there. I think we lucked out."

"Yes, you did. We're afraid they will shut down their operation if they think someone they don't know is snooping around. We've been watching Big Al's place but just can't prove anything. He's got a ton of cameras and a ton of security," she said.

"We saw it. Two of Big Al's guys removed, nicely I might add, the two we saw mug our friend on the pier," I said.

"This whole operation has Big Al's name all over it, especially with one of the Westlake girls."

"I thought Ashley was the good one. Do you think she was the one murdered by mistake?" I asked.

"That has had me wondering the same thing. My guess is Abby was in trouble, as usual, and came home for help from her sister. Ashley was always self-sufficient. She owned her own home out here on the island, supported herself with her own business, and occasionally, bailed Abby out of a mess," Officer Frederick said as background on the two women.

"Jess did tell us Ashley was the more reliable one," I said.

"Abby married some mob type right out of the fashion school they both attended in New York. According to Abby, if you listened to her side of the big business venture she had with her sister, she designed in New York and Ashley designed in Florida. Their business was Westlake Fashion. Abby said the New York side was where all the designs were sold. Ashley once told me, the only designs of hers in New York were the ones she made for Abby to wear. She did all her own marketing and sales in Florida. She had a good clientele and worked hard at it."

"The woman claiming to be Ashley said that Abby was here because her husband divorced her and she got nothing in a settlement. The woman said Abby came here with only herself, her clothes and her dog," I said.

"Jess suggested we talk to you. Before she found this," Jiff said as he held up the most recent flash drive, "she told us the two thugs were there and asked where Destin Harbor Marina, slip 108 was. She told them they were sitting in it. Brandy hadn't even found the fifth flash drive yet."

"We also make a connection to a number on this drive we believe to be a boat slip at that marina," I said. I thought leaving Jess out of the discovery of Big Al's World Famous Fishing Boat and dock box was a good idea if we discovered the info some other way. We had.

"We also can make a connection to a code on this drive, or at least we think we can," Jiff said. "We think the dates are for business or a job and the numbers have to do with payments. The initials are who to make the payment to, and the place to drop the money."

"The code we found on this drive matches an entry

with a date of this Wednesday. The code is DHM108 which is the number of slip with Big Al's Fishing Boat in it. The drops could be made in the dock box. That particular one has a large side with a combo lock and a smaller side with a keyed lock," I said.

"I'm astounded that code is on this drive, AND it belongs to Big Al's boat or dock box. He has, in the past, kept his hands clean from what I've seen," Officer Frederick said. "Something has changed with this one. His Tiki Bar and his strip clubs are the cash cows. I'm sure the FBI has been watching him if he's moving money across state lines. They take a keen interest if he hasn't paid or claimed any of it on his income taxes. I know someone who might tell us, if he's seen anything, and he sees it all. Brandy, are you up for some under-cover work?"

"Well, that depends," Jiff said. "Doing what?"

Officer Beverly Frederick milked this for all it was worth watching the two of us. I looked anxious but cautious and Jiff was already shaking his head no before he heard what she had in mind.

"Going to Big Al's…World Famous… All Male Review with Buns So Tight, you Wanna take a Bite?" she said. She could hardly keep from a big smile spreading all over her face.

"Wait, what?" I asked. "A male strip club?"

"No, not a male strip club, an All Male Review," she said. "They dance."

"I don't think so," Jiff said. "Brandy is too classy a

gal to put up with that."

"I appreciate your compliments and concern," I said to Jiff, but asked "Officer Frederick, why do we need to go undercover there?"

"Please call me Bev if we're gonna work together. By undercover, I need two gals to go in there like they're going for the show. I've had a guy working for that club going on two years. Besides, the extra money he makes, he keeps his eyes peeled for what goes on in the back of that bar. Big Al just made him the Manager, so if he didn't know what was going on before, he will now. Hot Rod will know what's going on with Big Al's boat in that marina."

"Hot Rod?" Jiff asked.

"Won't they suspect him?" I asked.

"Why is his name Hot Rod?" Jiff asked again.

"Stage name," Bev said to Jiff. To both of us, "We've had intel from our guy inside on drug deals and payoffs. But they seem to get tipped off or change locations at the last minute. This is now a murder investigation, so if there's a payoff associated with it, he may have heard or things have gotten a little more tense than usual. If what you two say is true, that it could be as soon as tomorrow or the day after, then he might be able to tell us. No one knows you there. You won't attract any attention."

"Okay, I'm in. Are you going with me? I'm not going alone, am I?" I said.

"I'll go with you," Jiff offered a little too quickly.

"No, you can't go. They won't go within a mile of her with you sitting there. Besides, no guys go to the All Male Review, not even gay ones. We need another hot chick," Bev said. "I'll call Jess. She'll do it." She picked up her phone to start the call and added, "Bring some dollar bills, some fives or tens—the bar will give you ones for change. Also, you will want to bring a twenty."

"Well, I know what the ones are for," I said rolling my eyes so only Jiff could see me, "But what's the twenty for, Rod's info?" I asked.

"No, he can't take money for information. He can only take tips for dancing. He works for the police. There's one male dancer you will want to tip a twenty to, and it's not Hot Rod," she said. "I know of what I speak. This dude has a bod like no one you've ever seen before, including your Mr. Hottie here, and he does a military act."

Jiff had counted out twelve ones from his wallet. He stopped when he heard someone might impress me enough to put a twenty in his G-String or whatever it is they wear.

"Don't worry about the twenty," I said to Jiff. "I don't think I'll need it."

"I don't this is a good idea on so many levels," Jiff said. He continued to count out his dollar bills saying, "I don't like this, I just don't like it."

"Jess is in," Bev said when she hung up her phone. She talked right over Jiff. "Y'all should be there tonight by ten p.m. Jess will send Hot Rod a message asking to get you two a good table. If he texts back, YOU GOT IT, we know he has info. If he says CAN'T THE PLACE IS SOLD OUT, we know he doesn't. She will pick you up here about nine-thirty tonight."

"I don't like this. None of this is a good idea. Wait a minute, did Brandy even commit to doing it?" Jiff looked rattled but hopeful I would say I didn't want to go. "You know you don't have to?"

"Jess knows Rod," Officer Bev said. "They both work for Big Al in his bars. She'll be fine, and I'll be in a squad car patrolling the area. Besides, who thinks twice about what these guys whisper in a gal's ear for a tip?"

Jiff's eyes widened.

"I'll be okay. We're just going to a club and wait for Hot Rod to give us any info he has and then we'll leave," I said. "Besides, what could go wrong?"

"Could it be this easy?" Officer Bev mused. "I hope you two can figure out that code. It looked like cities with marinas but there's other codes, we couldn't make sense of."

"I think some are gyms or maybe strip clubs," I said.

"We looked at those drives you gave Mike and started to think it might be boat slips but one had a number that doesn't match a slip. It was PBM9999," she said, "and there's no slip in the Pensacola Beach Marina with that number."

"That's because it was the end of the pier for big boats that can't fit into a regular slip, like a guest slip," I said. It was where Daniel had docked *In Your Dreams.*

Chapter Twelve

WHEN OFFICER BEV left, Jiff and I decided to drive over the bridge into Destin, rent a jet ski and hang out on Crab Island. This was a popular site for motor boats, jet skis or sailboats that could lift their keels. Crab Island wasn't an island at all but a shallow area boats all came to drop anchor and party. The water was about three feet deep so you could stop, get out, take a swim to cool off and walk around to meet friends on other boats. It was a giant, waist deep, water party. There was even a party barge that came prepared to grill fish sandwiches or hamburgers to sell for anyone who didn't pack a picnic lunch.

We could see what looked like fifty boats all at anchor and floating in the area on the north side of the bridge as we drove over it into Destin. A marina at the foot of the bridge rented jet skis and jet boats. Jiff rented one that looked like a glorified jet ski we both could get into and sit on seats rather than riding one behind the other. The jet boat allowed us to bring our picnic lunch with us. The principal of propulsion was the same as a jet ski.

I had packed sliced apples, celery, Monterey Jack cheese, crackers and some mixed nuts in separate plastic, snack-size bags, along with beer and wine in our small cooler. It wasn't much of a lunch, more of a big enough snack to hold us until dinner.

By the time we were underway in our jet boat, Jiff relaxed and started to smile and enjoy himself. He had me a bit worried because he wasn't happy about the all-male review, even though I said, it technically wasn't a strip club. I said I wouldn't like it if he was going to a Gentlemen's Club, but I trusted him. I reminded him I was there to get information, to look but not touch. He said he didn't sign on for me to look either.

We took a short ride from the marina out to the Gulf on the south side of the bridge. The waves were breaking at the channel opening and tossed us around a little. We decided to do what we came for and that was to hang out at the party flotilla to relax.

We putted in so as not to create a wake and found a spot near the party barge grilling fish sandwiches and hamburgers. It also was the area sound system and one Jimmy Buffet song after another blasted from the enormous speakers they had rigged on the barge. I overheard one guy on the boat next to us ask loudly if anyone with a boat owned any other CDs besides Buffet's. About ten people in earshot all answered "NO" at the same time.

Two labs were swimming around from boat to boat as if they had been appointed the welcome wagon. I worried they were tired and had no place to rest since their feet didn't hit the bottom. Then I saw one stop paddling his back feet and they sank to touched the bottom while he rested his front paws on the side of a boat. After a few minutes he took off swimming again. Finally, I saw both dogs swim back to the owner's boat. It had a wooden seat at water level so people could sit and the dogs could climb up and hop into their boat.

We walked around in the waist deep water, cooling off, drinking a glass of wine. I cut it off at one glass, because wine in the heat makes me sleepy and I had a long night ahead of me.

"Do you feel sufficiently sunburned by now?" Jiff asked as we wadded back to our two-man jet boat. We had gone through all the snacks, several bottles of water I packed and half of the bottle of Pinot Grigio we brought.

"Yes. I think we ought to head back. I saw a little seafood joint on the pier next to where we rented this boat. We could have an early dinner. There was a crowd there when we left the dock," I said. "That usually means they have good food."

"Good idea. I'm a little hungry, but I really didn't want to eat a fish sandwich from the party barge. Those dudes are all wasted from all the beer I watched them consume. Who knows how long that fish has been in the heat."

"I wonder how they are going to get back to their dock?"

"Not our problem," Jiff said. "That's what the Coast Guard gets paid big bucks for. I don't think they will call for help since the Coast Guard can fine them for a DUI, same as in a vehicle, or to tow them in. Staying right where they are would not be a bad place to sleep it off."

We walked next door to where we turned in our boat and waited for a table. It was an unpainted wood building with a screen area that separated the kitchen from the area where you walked in and placed your order. The kitchen was small but the menu was unbelievable. There was an enormous blackboard packed with anything you could want to eat. You could get any type of fish, crabs or shrimp made any way you liked—fried, grilled or boiled.

"What a find," Jiff said to me while he read the menu.

The line moved rather quickly and it smelled divine with the boiling spices mixing with the mouthwatering smell of fish frying. The kitchen was the only part of the establishment that could be secured. It was approximately fifteen feet by thirty feet with screens all the way around. Big wooden plank shutters were raised to let the fresh air flow in and the food smells flow out. It appeared to have running water because there were big sinks but the cooking was all done on moveable propane burners.

I ordered a grilled grouper sandwich and Jiff got a fried soft-shell crab sandwich. I noticed they were served on giant buns as a tray of orders went by us. We took our number and waited for a table to open up. All the tables were outside along two parallel piers connected at the ends. The piers were about ten feet apart and the middle allowed you to look down at the sea life passing underneath. I saw crabs, a needle fish, several minnows, small shiny fish, and a small ray, locally called a Skate swim by. There were barnacles all up and down the pilings under water.

Boats could come up and dock on the lower level piers connected by three or four steps to the restaurant level pier. We waited a few minutes until a picnic table with an umbrella opened up. We sat in the shade watching the sun dropping in the sky. A young girl brought our order in plastic baskets with the best sweet potato fries I think I've ever had.

Two seagulls who had been circling the piers landed on the rail nearest our table and stared at us. A waitress would shoo them off the rail when she passed, but they floated overhead and returned as soon as she walked away. As other diners finished and left taking their trays, the gulls kept an eye on our plates hoping we'd leave them something.

Several signs on the handrails where the birds were perched and on placards on the tables instructed us NEVER FEED THE BIRDS! A smaller inscription on the table placards instructed us further to bus our trays to the exit area. Sorry birds.

On the way back to the condo Jiff said he was worrying more and more over tonight. He thought the whole thing was a bad idea. I believed he really meant he was worrying more and more over me ogling nearly nude men dancing provocatively as the bad idea.

"How many single gals do you think go to these male dance clubs?" I asked.

"More than I care to think about," Jiff said.

"A lot," I said. "That means I'll just blend in with all the others."

Jiff rolled his eyes and said, "This isn't like going to the theatre where you sit back, watch a performance, then applaud. This is going to be more like those wrestling matches you see on TV. I don't think you are going to blend in at all. That's what scares me."

☙ ☙ ☙ ☙ ☙ ☙ ☙ ☙ ☙

JESS KNOCKED ON the door of the condo precisely at nine-thirty p.m. She wore makeup, an unbuttoned man's white dress shirt with a lacy tank top under it that showed a lot of cleavage, and a blue jean mini skirt. I didn't think anyone sold the big, dangling earrings she wore anymore. Her brunette, dark hair was styled to hang loose on her shoulders. I almost didn't recognize her from the bar. Her look in the bar had her in comfortable clothes, no makeup with hair pulled up and pinned to keep her neck cool.

"Wow, you look great," I said and shot her the look to notice Jiff sitting at the bar in the condo.

"Thanks," was all she said, picking up on not returning a compliment.

"I'm ready, just let me grab my purse."

"Hey Jiff, I'll have her home in a couple of hours. We just need to hook up with Hot Rod and hear what he has to tell us. He doesn't want to risk too many phone calls."

Don't say *hook up*, I thought. Jiff was being as nice as he could be. I could tell he was not happy about me going to a male strip club…correction…all male review, and leaving him home, alone.

"I'll be back before you know it," I said and gave him a hug and a kiss. "Let's go."

"She'll be home and looking for love," Jess said laughing as we walked out.

Stop talking, I mentally put my hand over her mouth.

At the car she said, "You look nice, I didn't want to say too much in front of your boyfriend."

"Thanks." I had on a white leather halter top and a black pair of linen pants.

"Here, this is a purple color hair spray, use some on your hair. Just put one or two stripes around your face. That looks best," she said handing me a can of something.

"I don't want to put that in my hair. What if I can't get it out?"

"It washes out. We'll stop in the ladies' room at a gas station and you can use it in there. You don't want anyone to recognize you, right? That will help. It's out of character for you but most of the women in there will have something like this going on."

"Okay," I said and she handed me earrings that looked like the lost cousins to hers.

"Put those on."

"Why? I'm wearing earrings."

"Yours look like diamond studs and I'm trying to get you to blend in more with the way the rest of the audience will look," Jess said.

"Why? Are we dancing on stage too?"

"No, this is an all-male club, you know that."

"That was a joke," I said.

We stopped at a gas station on the way and I streaked my blonde hair with purple hair spray and Jess had a can of pink she put in hers. On the way back to the car, she pulled out a bunch of bangle bracelets for me to put on. She gave me some big, flashy, rings to wear and had a pair of very large framed eyeglasses she wanted me to put on.

"Are these someone's prescription glasses? How will I see?"

"No, they were mine but when the lens got too weak, I changed them out to Transition lens. These go from clear to sunglasses—no prescription. I wear contacts now but I liked the frames and use them as sunglasses. They cost a fortune.

"I bet they did. These are Jimmy Choo frames," I said looking at them closely. I couldn't help thinking if he makes super expensive shoes, why wouldn't he make super expensive frames for eyeglasses?

"The frames will be clear inside and they're super comfy."

"Yeah, they are comfy," I said putting them on. "I might have to look into getting a pair of these." Then I thought she probably paid as much for these as I pay in rent every month.

"If anyone shines a light in your face they will start to darken. Not that I think anyone would recognize you in that get-up. Fluff up your hair and put on more lipstick. Do you have any that's red?"

"No."

"Look in my purse. There's a clear cosmetic bag with some in it. The name is Light My Fuego. Use it," she said pulling into the parking lot.

There it was. Big Al's World Famous All Male Review—Buns So Tight—You Wanna Take a Bite! That was written all over a shipping container situated at an angle at the front of the lot adjacent to the street so you couldn't miss it. The building was lit up in white lights, around the door, around the roof, around the shipping container, everywhere.

"This looks like someone put Hollywood in a Trailer Park," I said.

"All celebrities have trailers on movie sets. Hollywood already *is* a Trailer Park," Jess said. "Look, when we get in there, it will be loud and hard to talk. Text me if you need to tell me something really important."

"How will we hear Rod?" I asked.

"He gets close enough for you to hear him," Jess smiled a wicked smile. "Don't worry, you'll hear him or anyone who wants to talk to you." She used the finger quote thing when she said talk. "But text any question on your phone you want to ask Rod. Be brief and let him see it. He'll tell you the answer in your ear. Keep your phone in your lap but tone down the backlight. If any of the security guys come nosing around, turn it over in your lap or use the flashlight app like you're looking for something you dropped on the floor. Women do that all the time in there."

"Okay." Jess started to open her car door. "Wait," I said. "What if I have to give some guy a tip, I mean, how do I give one of the dancers a tip? What is the protocol for that?"

"Just throw it at them, hand it to them or stick it in their G-string if they point at it."

"I don't want to stick money in anything. How about I give it to you to put in their, in their…whatever?"

"No, that won't work. You'll look like a weirdo or something."

"I don't want to accidently touch…touch them or…touch anything," I said.

"Don't worry about that. They want you to touch them. These are male strippers, not women. They," (she pointed at Big Al's building with both index fingers) "want us" (she pointed at the two of us) "to touch them" (she pointed with both index fingers below her waist). Its women strippers who don't want any bozo grabbing them.

"These guys can handle themselves if some patron starts to get rowdy, even if it's a really, really, big gal," Jess said and laughed at me. "All the women in there want to jump these guys, so act like that or you're gonna stand out. Besides, wait until you see the bouncers. They can pick somebody up with one hand."

"Wait, I don't want to touch anyone and I don't want anyone touching me," I said. She locked the car and headed for the entrance.

"Here we go," she said waving her hand in a circle over her head ignoring me.

We made our way past a line of women giving us the evil eye waiting to get in to the bouncer's checkpoint. I was about to pull out the cover charge when Jess shook her head no. She leaned in close to the guy and said something in his ear and then she tapped to the clipboard in his hand. The guy at the door was very big, six foot six at least, had a bald head, which I think is a thing right now. He was muscular, his arms were covered in those razor blade looking tats, which I also think is a thing right now. His hands looked like he could palm a basketball, or someone's head, even if it was a really, really big head. This must have been what Jess meant when she said these dudes can pick someone up with one hand. This guy was a big, scary man.

It took him a few seconds to find Jess' name, even after she looked at the clipboard with him, found her name and finally pointed it out to him. There must have been a notation because after he saw her name his face came up looking marginally less bored than he did when we walked up. He removed the velvet rope to let us pass, reconnected it and said, "Right this way, ladies. There's a reserved table for you up front."

Was this guy new? He didn't seem to recognize Jess and I thought all Big Al's employees knew each other. I'd have to ask her or text her. That could wait. First, I wanted to meet this Hot Rod guy and get the info he wanted to relay back to Bev, and then leave.

Once inside, I had to watch where I was going. It was dark in there except for the colored lights that were zipping around in crazy circles from the ceiling and moving like mini search lights. A light would momentarily stop, light a six-inch circle on the floor in front of me, and then, zip, it was gone and it was dark again. The music was at a normal level to allow the waiters to take drink orders and for Jess and me to have limited conversation. It required leaning into each other and raising our voices but we could still hear each other.

Out of the corner of my eye I spotted a waiter headed our way with two glasses of champagne on his tray. I thought it might be Hot Rod. When he started to put them down in front of us, I wasn't paying attention to him and was looking for my iPhone in my purse. I noticed he was wearing Lycra tuxedo pants, no shirt, and a white collar with a bow tie. His body appeared to be spray tanned.

"Good evening, Ladies, my name is Joe and I'll be your waiter until it's time for me to dance and entertain you. These are compliments of Hot Rod," he said.

I started to look up at him as he was setting down our drinks but never got past his six pack. Even though I've spent my fair share of time in a gym, I had never seen a body like his. I watched him walk away from out table. His body was perfect. It felt like someone turned on the heat in here. I was having one of those impure thoughts the nuns were always warning us about in the catholic school. I started thinking I'd have no qualms about putting a bill in that guy's G-String.

After he left Jess leaned over and said, "I bet you're sorry you didn't bring more twenties, right?"

"Wait. What? If that's the guy everyone gives twenty-dollar bills to, I can see why? He's like a Greek god."

"And more. Wait until you see him dance. I wanna give him a twenty for just walking up to our table," she said still looking in the direction he walked off in.

"Is there an ATM machine in here?" I asked looking around.

"No, you have to come prepared. Bev warned you."

I thought I had at least one twenty in my wallet I didn't tell Jiff about. He sent me on my mission with about thirty or so one-dollar bills I thought I could exchange for a twenty at the bar. He said he would count them when I got back. Funny guy. He'd faint if he knew I was looking for twenties in my wallet right now.

A few minutes later another guy in a real tux, complete with a shirt, was working his way over to us while glad handing women at tables. He was good looking but he didn't have the same effect on me as our waiter had. After I saw our waiter, I knew I could only have bills for him.

When Mr. Tuxedo got to our table, he pulled up a chair, sat down opposite us and asked if we liked our drinks. He had the most perfect white smile any toothpaste ad would die to have on their billboard.

"Hot Rod, this is my cousin, Mandy from Arkansas. Mandy, this is Hot Rod, the manager of all this," Jess said smiling. My peripherals could see her watching me during the introductions. I didn't react to the cover she made up for my name and relationship to her. Maybe she came up with it on the spot, or maybe she already knew she would use it but didn't bother filling me in.

"It's a pleasure," I said not knowing what an Arkansas accent sounds like. Jess must have thought mine would pass so I just went with it. "Thank you for the champagne, it's all I ever drink."

"Well, any cousin of Jess is a cousin of mine, if anyone asks. Nice specs," he said and flashed those pearly whites again. He put his arm around my shoulder and nuzzled his face into my hair. "You smell good."

The women in here were gonna swoon. Heck, I was starting to feel giddy myself from the way he looked at me and that easy smile he gave. This guy was a born charmer.

"It's gonna be packed tonight," he said to Jess. "We have three hen parties in here."

He nodded to the tables behind us that I assumed he meant to be groups of women for bridal showers.

"You got a bunch of horny women in here tonight. You should make good tips," Jess said.

"They should distract anyone noticing you two, but try to act like you're into it. Big Al's here tonight, in the back. He's meeting someone and doesn't want to be bothered. They'll come out later and hang at the bar."

"Any idea who it is?" I asked.

"It's the guy he uses to move money. I overheard Al talking on the phone earlier saying, "Come here tonight. The heat has been turned up since that girl was murdered. We need to move up the time and change the drop location.'"

"The girl?" I leaned onto the table on my elbows moving closer to Rod like I was flirting. "He didn't use her name?"

Rod leaned in and took one of my hands and covered them with both of his. Then he raised one of my hands to his face and I thought he was going to kiss it. Instead, he licked it which I found disgusting. I started to wipe it off on my pants under the table when he let go of it.

"No names. He's careful." He got up to leave our table. He was still holding my other hand, extending his arm until our hands dropped apart, dramatically, like he was leaving for the front to fight in some war. "I'll be back for you," he dramatically mouthed to me and then threw a kiss so everyone in the place would notice.

I had to smile to myself. Yep, I bet he says that to all the girls. He moved on to the group of giggling women right behind us. They had several tables pushed together and one was wearing a paper tiara that said, BRIDE. There were several gift bags on the table, all very small. When I looked around, there were two more tables with small gift bags and two more women wearing paper tiaras that said BRIDE.

"This is rather an untraditional venue for a bridal shower," I said to Jess.

"You'd be surprised at the number of my friends who have had their wedding parties here. I've been to several. It's a lot more fun than sitting around with a bunch of catty women playing stupid games and drinking punch."

"They even bring gifts?" I asked. "Those bags are really small. What type of gifts do you bring to a party like this?" I wondered if the small bags all contained gift certificates.

"Oh, it's probably oils, lubricants, crotch-less undies for him or her. Something like that," Jess said.

Jiff was right about me and this place. It was sleazy. I wanted to leave…I wanted to leave right after I saw Mr. Twenty-Dollar Bill dance.

Jess was watching our waiter as he delivered drinks to the bridal party behind us. "I wouldn't mind the Twenty-Dollar man as my personal waiter, bringing drinks only to me, at a party in my honor. If I deserved preferential treatment, I'd want him to deliver it."

"Talk to Hot Rod," I said. "I bet if you let him lick your hand, or you lick his, he could make it happen for you."

I really couldn't see my mother or Jiff's mother being up for this kind of party to celebrate upcoming nuptials. My mother insisted I ruined the family name by moving out of our home without being married or chaperoned. Chaperoned? Did she think we were the Rockefellers? Imagine what she'd say about this in lieu of a traditional wedding shower especially if I opened a gift with his and her lube.

My mother gave my sister a pass even though she was very pregnant when she married, but she was still living at home. She actually believed she could keep my sister's six-month pregnant body a secret at the wedding all because she still lived under their roof. If anyone should have had a chaperone it was my sister.

Since I grew up next door to Dante, both families always expected us to marry. Dante's mother, Miss Ruth, would participate in anything, this included, if I had agreed to marry her son. She had to settle for my sister marrying one of Dante's brothers. The one that was the baby daddy.

Chapter Thirteen

THE SHOW WAS about to start according to someone with a Mr. Microphone making announcements, from backstage. There was no one out front that I could see trying to get everyone's attention and the voice sounded a lot like Hot Rod's. He told us the time we all had been waiting for had come. The music blasted louder along with women screaming following that announcement. When the screaming died down, Mr. Microphone said Hot Rod would be the first to take the stage. He knew how to rev up the fun and get this party started.

The women went wild screaming again. When the screaming died down an octave, Mr. Microphone went on to cover the club rules—no jumping on tables or onto the stage during a performance, no grabbing the dancers… really? He announced a few more brainless instructions that anyone with an ounce of sense should already have learned as basic, common courtesy. This met with a fair amount of booing.

I thought. *Jiff was right. This is more like a wrestling match.*

The audience was further informed they could only throw tips on stage, hand tip money to the dancer or, respectfully—*REALLY*—tuck any bills inside their costume if the dancer was at your table, and indicated it was acceptable. Under no circumstances were audience members allowed throw their own items of clothing onto the stage, pull off the dancers' costumes or they would be removed from the premises.

I guessed the guy who met us at the door would be the one to remove someone from the premises. I looked around, and no one had a head even close to the size of a basketball. Easy night.

Later, I realized 'at your table' means 'in your face' at your table. When he said, "Sit back, relax and get ready for a night of sexual abandonment," every woman in the place—I was forced to stand or look out of place—jumped to their feet and the screaming started again. The bridal group behind us seemed to be making the most noise.

Suddenly, the lights were racing across the stage which was no more than three feet off the floor with a T-shaped runway extending about ten feet into the crowded room of tables. Our table was dead center of the stage, closest to the foot of the runway. Dancers could step off the stage and be at our table.

The sound system roared like a car engine being revved at the Indy 500. The sound continued to increase until it got to a decibel point that could cause permanent hearing loss. My ears hurt so I put my fingers in them to drown out the noise. Jess knocked my hand closest to her away from my ear. She gave me a stern look my mother used to give me when I was doing some unacceptable behavior, like in this instance, trying to keep myself from going deaf.

The curtains flew open and there was Hot Rod sitting behind the steering wheel of a stage prop Mustang convertible—front only—wearing a mechanics jumpsuit. Only this jumpsuit was Lycra. Skin tight Lycra. He jumped out of the Mustang, did an impressive spin and landed flat on his back on a Craftsman Creeper, the kind mechanics use to roll under vehicles. My dad had one of those and he loved it.

Rod rolled under the Mustang, and when he came out the other side he used his feet to spin around while he remained lying on the Creeper, doing some gyrations I don't believe my dad knew could be done on one of those. I certainly never imaged anyone does those things on the Creeper all the times I saw it in our garage leaning against the wall.

Hot Rod was pumping, grinding or gyrating to Sammy Hagar's *I Can't Drive 55* and acting like he was repairing the car in between hip thrusts until he pulled off his flyaway jumpsuit and danced out to the T part of the stage. The curtains closed behind him. Nothing much between Rod and the audience but his smile and a small piece of Lycra working its magic with the women.

Jess leaned into my ear and yelled so loud it made

my ear buzz, "Yell, clap, throw some bills at him. You're sitting there like a bump on a cucumber." She was discreetly trying to pour her drink out under our table but it was landing on my foot.

I immediately clapped, yelled and did a wolf whistle and dug some ones out of my purse. Most women were trying to get his attention by doing lewd things to lure him to their table. Didn't the thought cross their minds that there might be cameras in here? Certainly, their friends could blackmail them by taking videos on their cell phone cameras. No telling where those could wind up.

Hot Rod danced out to the end of the runway and teased the crowd pointing at different tables to see who yelled the loudest or made the most provocative moves for him to dance over to. I was rummaging in my purse looking for the one-dollar bills when his legs straddled over either side of mine all the while doing hips thrusts. It looked like he was trying to have sex with the air.

I tried to hand him a few bills, but he pointed to his costume, and here I use the term, costume, as the description for lack of what it really looked like... dental floss. OMG! He wanted me to put the money in his G-string.

Women were throwing bunched up bills at him and they were raining down on my head and some fell on the stage. I finally folded the bills in fourths and aimed to slide them in the Lycra string at his hip. Oh no. He grabbed my hand before I could put the bills there and pointed to the front of his costume. The women screamed even louder, "Do it! Do it!"

I looked at Jess who nodded toward Hot Rod standing there. I just pulled out the front of what he was wearing with a fingernail, closed my eyes, and tucked in the bills as fast as I could with two fingers on my other hand.

Rod took my hand and provocatively licked it which only made the women scream louder if that was possible. Then he went to gyrate at the table behind us while I discreetly wiped my hand off on my pants under the table, again.

I thought, *Oh brother! This info I came here for better be worth it.*

I continued to clap, and wolf whistle. Screaming like I was locked in a warehouse full of Zombies coming to attack me did not come natural for me like it seemed to for most of the women in here. Jess started screaming a la trapped by Zombies in a warehouse.

Finally, Hot Rod cruised on back to the stage with more dollar bills than I thought his costume would accommodate. Lycra is truly a wonder fabric. The cheering women rose to a standing ovation. He did one more hip thrust at the crowd, then disappeared behind the curtain while some other dancers came out and collected his tips from the stage, tables and floor.

Mr. Mic, the endearment I began to call the announcer to myself, was describing the next man of muscle to drive us wild. He was the All American man you wanted on our military team, G.I. Joe. He described him as one who had "Special Forces" all women could appreciate. I hoped this wasn't going to be our very own special agent, Mike Perricone. Probably not, since he didn't refer to him as Magic Mike, Surfer Boy or Baywatch. Mr. Mic went on to introduce G.I. Joe as the military man who knew what full engagement meant and believed in full body contact. Watch out ladies!

I would have to admit, if I was being truthful, I was anxious to see more of that waiter. When the curtain opened, there were several pieces of workout equipment on stage. There were a couple of barbells, a flat bench with a bar, some free weights, and a chin up or pull-up bar on a stand. G.I. Joe had his back to us—it was a really nice back. He was painted in camouflage body paint from his head to his feet. He did have on some sort of camouflage G-string and combat boots. He looked nude, like he was wearing only body paint and no clothes. Well, he wasn't wearing much in the way of clothing. The boots were not tied.

When the music from the movie Top Gun played Danger Zone, he jumped up and did a couple of pull ups. I could see every muscle ripple down his back to his legs. I think Big Al's slogan came from this guy's buns. He had buns so tight… well, you remember the slogan. Whoever put these dance numbers together didn't have a clear understanding of what the different military divisions actually did. G. I.'s refer mostly to the Army and Top Gun was about the Air Force.

Who really cared? I was already wolf whistling and yelling for more. He kicked off the boots and pulled his feet up to his chest, over his head and through his arms all the while holding onto the chin-up bar. He proceeded to do upside down pull ups. I had never seen anything like it in any gym I've ever been to. I couldn't take my eyes off of his body. I watched every move he made and every muscle flex. I could have sat there and watched him do upside down pull ups for the rest of my natural life.

The crowd went wild, and I was impressed enough to add a couple of extra wolf whistles. Secretly, I hoped he'd come to the end of the runway so I could have a closer, more personal view of him. I took a sneak peek at Jess who was nodding and moving around in her seat with the music. Her eyes were glued to this guy. She had a twenty in one hand. I thought I better get out my twenty and be ready when he comes by our table. I wouldn't want to miss my chance to have him stand over me a little extra time.

He worked his way down the end of the runway and hopped down and started accepting the twenty-dollar bill tips. No one would touch him because of the body paint. When he got to our table, he was doing some hip thrusting action Hot Rod must have taught him.

When I finally looked up at his face, I caught a profile and then he turned and I saw him head on.

Wait… what?

It was Wallace—our super polite, All American husband, father, Security Guard at Jiff's condo building who was, indeed, in the military stationed at Hurlburt Field with a wife, two children and one on the way.

I felt like I had plunged into an ice bath. Any impure thoughts I had of G.I. Joe had gone into a deep freeze. OMG! The second shock wave that followed my recognition of Wallace was what if he recognized me?

I started to come to terms with the shock of his identity and now felt cornered sitting dead center in the room. I felt every ounce of shame the years in a catholic school system heaped on me for ogling him, and for being in a place like this in the first place. OMG! He was gyrating his way right up to our table. He was bound to look at me. Someone who knew me would recognize me in this get up if they looked in my face. I held my head down, flashed my iPhone camera like I was taking a picture so the Transition lens would darken, and put my hand out with the twenty-dollar bill acting like I was looking for something I dropped on the floor with my phone light. I noticed the Transition lens darkening.

I felt him take the twenty from my hand and say, "Thank you, Ma'am."

Yep, it was Wallace. No mistake.

I wanted to go home and take a shower.

I looked up when he had already moved to the next table. I felt an arm slide around my shoulder and Hot

Rod had joined us again, sitting between Jess and me. He was back wearing his tuxedo.

"Are you enjoying the show?" he whispered in my ear. He raised his hand at a passing waiter and made the universal circular motion indicating another round of champagne.

I nodded as enthusiastically as I could with the most fake smile I could muster.

"Look at the bar," Rod was nuzzling my hair with his face so I could hear him and no one could see him talking. "That's Al and the guy he had the meeting with. They won't stay long, one drink, that's it."

While I played along with Rod smiling and wiggling around in my seat like a schoolgirl, I twisted to see who was at the bar. Well, this was a night for surprises. First, Wallace and now, I saw Daniel Becnel at the bar with a man that I recognized as Big Al from the Facebook photo on Ashley Westlake's page. Besides the male dancers, bartenders and waiters, they were the only other men in the place—the only men not wearing Lycra or a tuxedo. Daniel had his back mostly to the crowd, and he wasn't looking in my direction.

"Who is the man with Big Al? Do you know him?" I cuddled up to Hot Rod asking in his ear.

"No name, but he's the man who moves money for Al. He's got a big, fast sailboat and access to all of Al's cigarette boats up and down the coast," Rod said. He started to get up, holding my hand as if he dreaded saying goodbye like he was leaving again for another foreign war. He leaned down, and I thought he was going to kiss my hand this time, but instead, he licked it. Again.

I texted Jess:

2 men in here know me, and 1 is at the bar w/ Al.

She didn't look calm. I felt terrified. She glanced at my phone and nodded. Then we both went back to watching the next dancer out who was, by no means, competition for Wallace, aka G.I. Joe or Hot Rod. We saw what we came to see, and I was pretty sure we had all the info Hot Rod could pass along. I was ready to high tail it out of there.

Jess texted me, *Ready when you are*

There was no bill for us so we left two twenty-dollar bills on the table with a note that read, for G.I. Joe—our Waiter.

We gave our second round of the two untouched glasses of Champagne to the Bride at the table behind us. I drank one glass of cheap champagne and Jess maybe had a couple of sips.

Back in the car, Jess said, "You know what I've always wondered about when I come out of a place like that?"

"I can't imagine. What?"

"Men are such creatures of comfort, I always wonder how they can wear those G-Strings or those thong suits. You know how uncomfortable underwear like that is?"

"After everything we saw in there, that's what you came out wondering?" I asked her. "G.I. Joe—our waiter and the man I lusted after when I saw him without a shirt—is a very nice Security Guard in Jiff's building, married with two kids, and another one on the way."

"Oh, don't worry about him. If Rod sent him over to wait on us, he trusts him. Besides, he didn't look surprised when he saw you. I told you that get up would work."

"That really isn't my point. I feel kinda sleazy having looked at him the way I did," I said.

"You're kidding, right? Men do it. We're as human as they are," she said and looked non-pulsed.

"I wonder what his pregnant wife thinks, if she even knows he's doing this. He told us he worked security at the condos for extra money," I said.

"Maybe he practices his moves at home. It might be why she's pregnant with their third child, ever think of that?"

"No, I guess I didn't," I said.

"His wife is probably thrilled with the extra cash if they have three kids on a military salary," she said. "Did you get anything from Rod? I saw him nuzzling you. That's when he passes info."

"Yes, and one thing I didn't want to know."

"If it's about any of Big Al's businesses, you need to discuss it with Bev," Jess said. "I try to know very little of what he does or is into. I try to ignore any and all of his goings on to maintain plausible deniability as Bev puts it."

Chapter Fourteen

J ESS ASKED ME to call Officer Bev on the way back to the condo to meet us there. As I made the call, a flashing blue light came up behind our car and the loudspeaker told us to pull over. We had just left the parking lot. We barely were going twenty miles per hour. Jess pulled off the highway into another business parking lot that was well lit.

Bev answered her cell phone as one of the patrolmen turned on the siren.

"Bev, Jess is being pulled over on Highway 98. We just left the Male Review. We are pulling over into the Olive Garden Restaurant parking lot," I said.

"I'll be right there," she said. "Don't hang up. Leave this line open."

Two big, overweight cops were getting out of their car and walking up either side of Jess' car.

"Step out of the vehicle with your hands up," one said to Jess.

"You too, Blondie," the other one said to me.

"Officer, what are we being pulled over for?" I asked ever so politely.

"We think you got cocaine on you or in your car," the one on Jess' side said.

Just then, Bev pulled into the parking lot and rolled down her window and asked the one on my side, "What's going on?"

"Stay out of this. We got it," my side said.

"Sorry, but if you're going to search them or the car, I'm going to stay here so I can testify it's a good search. She's my sister," Bev said nodding to Jess. "She's our cousin," she said nodding at me. "Neither one is gonna have anything narcotic on them. So, if you're gonna search either of them or the car, I'm gonna be present as a witness just so there's no misunderstanding." She started to get out of her patrol car.

The two looked at each other and the cop on Jess' side said, "Get outta here," to us. To Bev, "I hope you remember this when it's one of us who needs a pass."

"No pass involved. They're not holding anything. Go ahead and look," she said and took out a gigantic handheld flashlight that had to be two feet long—a wicked-looking laser with eye-blinding candlepower.

"Well, you might think about minding your own business, then," the one on my side told her as they got back into their vehicle.

"Maybe I need to call the Captain and do a search of all of our vehicles right here. Wanna wait for him?" Bev asked.

They didn't answer. They drove off in a hurry.

"What was that all about?" I asked. "Were we gonna be set up?"

"Looks like it. Those two have more drug busts than everyone else put together, and I've heard it rumored it's because they find stuff that's not there until they look. It could be you ruffled someone's feathers in Big Al's," Bev said.

"I don't think so," Jess said, "but Brandy said she knew two guys in there and one was meeting with Big Al."

"Let's get back to your condo and talk about this. I don't want Jess hearing any more than she has to. I'll be there a few minutes after you. I have to stop for gas."

JESS AND I were met with a strange look from Jiff until I remembered we had the pink and purple stripes in our hair along with some flashy earrings, bracelets and blood red lipstick.

"All this," I said sweeping my hand up and down from my head to my feet, "was so I'd fit in and not draw attention to myself."

"That look kept you from drawing attention to yourself?" he looked flabbergasted.

"You had to be there," I said and Jess nodded. "What's important is who else was there. And you won't guess."

Waiting on Jiff to recover from our updated appearance which was taking a little longer than I thought, I went to the door and Officer Bev Frederick was on the other side about to knock when I opened it.

"Hey," she said to everyone in general.

"We were just going to tell him what we found out, and what happened. It's a good thing you're here too so we don't have to repeat it," I said.

"I didn't think I wanted Jess here since she could have plausible deniability. Did Rod give you the info?" she asked me.

"See I told you she'd say that," Jess said to me.

I nodded.

"Well, after that bogus stop to search, I don't think you'll be working for Big Al anymore," Bev said to Jess.

"Why not? You don't think he sent those two goons?" Jess asked.

"What two goons? What stop?" Jiff asked looking from face to face to see if anyone would give him an answer.

"If Big Al saw you in there, on a night he was having a meet with someone, I bet he would suspect you were working for me," Bev said. "Or that she's working for us." Bev nodded at me.

"We saw him in there, at the bar," Jess said. "I didn't think he saw me but my name was on the VIP list. Hot Rod put it on there so we'd get right in."

"You won't believe who was with Big Al in there," I said to Jiff.

"Please start at the beginning and only one of you talk at a time," Jiff said. "Please?"

"Jess and I got there and everything was fairly normal, well, normal for an All Male Review. Rod came by and told me that Big Al was in the back meeting with someone who moves his money around for the drops. He said he overheard Al talking about changing a drop time and location since the girl was murdered and there was heat. He didn't know his name and that they would be out after they concluded their business to have a drink at the bar. Rod also said, they wouldn't stay long, only one drink. Male dancers aren't their thing."

Jiff rolled his eyes.

"That's exactly what they did. Big Al and another guy came out and Brandy texted me she knew two men in the place and one was with Big Al," Jess said.

"Who was it?" Jiff asked me.

"Daniel," I answered almost ready to burst with the information.

"No, you must be wrong," he said.

"It was definitely Daniel," I said to him. Turning to Jess and Bev, I asked if one of them could tell Jiff about the two cops that pulled us over. I needed a quiet minute to process some of this. "I'm going to the ladies' room."

In the quiet of the bathroom, I laid down on the marble floor. It was cool and calming. It allowed the tension to dissolve out of my body so I could think. The facts I had all seemed to stack like pancakes but nothing was in order. Everything seemed out of place.

What had been bothering me was Daniel.

Daniel having Rascal seemed like too big of a coincidence. Then the two guys turn up when we're away at dinner to mug him. He conveniently happened to be on the end of the pier waiting for us so they could find him easily. These facts had been gnawing on me since that next morning when we took Daniel back to his yacht and Ashley/Abby was waiting for us. Now, I needed to figure out how she was involved with Daniel and Big Al.

I have always believed that our parallel universes bounce off each other, cross over one another or collide when there's a good reason for them to. Maybe one person is in a universe doing something. Another person in another universe is doing something related and can help figure it out if we shared the same space even if it's only for a nanosecond. I was waiting for the collision with a helpful universe.

Since we found the dead girl on the beach, I felt like my atoms were orbiting in my head trying to find the ones they were supposed to line up with. To make a molecule, or in my case, a complete thought.

Jiff was pacing when I came out the bathroom.

"This is exactly what I was afraid of," he said. "These guys are not playing around. You could have had a felony charge on you two tonight and jail time if this played out."

I hated when he was right. I hated it even more when he scared me by being right. This wasn't a good time to tell him he was also right about the male review audience being similar to a wrestling match crowd.

"How well can you trust Mike Perricone?" I asked Bev. "I know he's a glory hound but do you think he's clean?"

"I can't prove he's done any wrong doing, and he's a giant pain in the tuchus," Bev said. "I just don't trust him."

"Well, I don't think we should give him the last flash drive I found," I said to Jiff. "Even if we tell him what happened and who I saw, I doubt it will make him more considerate of our help."

"I wouldn't count on him to act any differently than he did the last time you gave him something you found," Bev said. "I've got a better idea. This is over Perricone's pay grade, anyway. Mine too."

Bev put in a call to her Captain, who called his FBI counterpart who told her he was coming to meet all of us himself to see what had developed.

Chapter Fifteen

Area Director Steve Sorenson knocked on our condo door several times before he woke one of us up. It was two-thirty a.m. into Tuesday. We all fell asleep in the living room waiting on his arrival. With him was Bev's Captain, Claire Duffy with the Police Department.

Bev gave the Area Director and Captain an overview from how we all met when Jiff and I discovered the body, found Rascal, and what we heard and saw tonight at the All Male Review. I thought sparks would fly when the Area Director asked why Bev would enlist the help of civilians, meaning me.

Bev was calm, said we both did similar work to help the New Orleans Police Department from time to time. We found the body and the dog along with the flash drives. Now, I had a good idea of what the codes on those drives meant.

"Here's what I found inside Rascal's collar that was hidden under the clasp," I held out my hand with the last flash drive. "The other sleeve I found and gave to Mike Perricone was rather obvious. This flash drive was separate from those and harder to notice. The data on this one seems more current," I said.

"More current, how?" Steve Sorenson asked.

"Well, for one thing, the date for what I assume is the payoff for the recent murder was not logged as paid. It does, however, have a drop location and an amount. It was Al Flashpole's dock box for his Big Al's Fishing Boat in the Destin Harbor Marina. It looks like DHB108 on this file for Wednesday."

"There were at least five other entries with no dates, but with the drop off locations and amounts. I think you have to watch them or go to them and open those lockers or dock boxes to find the money," Jiff said.

"So, we take the money, then what?" Sorenson asked. "We can't prove its money for a hit or payoff."

"We sit on the locations and see who comes looking for it. Or, we wait and see who comes looking for Big Al for not paying up," Captain Claire Duffy said.

"That's what I was thinking," I said. "I think Big Al is the contact with Abby's ex-husband. He has Daniel pick up money from him or some other place, maybe the Caymans, and put it in a drop location. I don't think Daniel knows the particulars."

"Daniel?" both Sorenson and Duffy asked.

"Daniel Becnel. He owns a big, fast, catamaran, has access to all of Big Al's cigarette boats and he's the one Hot Rod pointed out to me at the All Male Review. He said he moves Big Al's money," I said. "Rod didn't know his name, but I did. I would bet you find the money in those locations in a black, Patagonia, waterproof duffle bag. He had a stack of them in a cabinet on his yacht."

"You were on this guy's yacht?" Captain Claire Duffy asked.

"I booked an evening sail with him," Jiff answered. "Turns out we knew each other from law school in New Orleans. He told me he travels around booking trips on his catamaran from here to the islands now. He no longer practices law in New Orleans."

I nodded in agreement and added, "We sailed with him Saturday night, the night he was mugged, and he told us he was leaving for the BVI Sunday morning. I just saw him with Big Al in the All Male Review. He's not in the BVI."

"How do we find this guy, Daniel and his boat?" Captain Duffy asked.

"The name of his seventy-seven-foot catamaran is *In Your Dreams,*" Jiff said.

"Daniel claims he files a sail plan with the Coast Guard," I said. "It might be worthwhile to see if he's filed one out of Pensacola to the BVI, or to any other marina around here. It was not in a slip in the Pensacola Marina because his catamaran is too big. He was at the end of pier nine and there was a notation on this flash drive that read PBH9999. If he wasn't in a numbered slip, that's the code for a guest slip at the end of a pier. The Harbormaster would have to confirm where he could dock in the marina. That goes for any marina. I took it to mean someone was supposed to meet him there."

"He certainly moves around in plain sight if he's on a big yacht and calling in a sail plan with the Coast Guard," Sorenson said.

"Well, it makes him look legit. A guy with a big boat like that might keep a lot of cash with him in case of emergencies if he's down in the islands. A boat that size can't be cheap to fill up or get a part for," Captain Duffy said. She added, "My family has had every kinda sailboat you can imagine, and none of them are cheap to repair. Every foot of a boat's length adds exponentially to the upkeep and fuel it takes to operate one."

"I'd like to get one of the agents in cyber-crime to take a look at this with the both of you. Ms. Alexander, Mr. Heinkel, would you mind?" Sorenson asked.

"Not at all. We'd be happy to do it later today. We're supposed to leave tomorrow," I said answering for the two of us. I knew Jiff did not want to do this. He wanted to spend what little vacation we had left, vacationing.

"We can add a day or two if needed," Jiff said. "Brandy has to be back in New Orleans by Friday."

"I'll have someone contact you…" he looked at his watch and said, "later today, around ten a.m. If that's okay?"

Jiff and I nodded. A few hours' sleep was about all we were going to get until they sent the tech over from Cyber Crimes, but an hour sounded good right now.

We said goodbye to Bev, Jess, Captain Duffy and Area Director Sorenson. On the way out, Bev and her captain lagged behind.

"If you don't mind, we'd like to contact you further on this if we need some help finding this Daniel and his yacht," Captain Duffy said.

"Sure, anything you need," I said and then asked Bev, "Did you ever hear from Ashley Westlake again after I said she showed up at that pier Sunday morning?"

"No, why?"

"No reason. I just wondered if she's still around," I said. "I think she's Abby Westlake, and her sister, Ashley was the one accidently killed in her place." I looked at Officer Bev and said, "You would know the difference, right?"

"Maybe, but I haven't seen either one in years. Jess would be better at telling them apart," she said.

"Why do you think that?" Captain Duffy asked me.

"Just something about the way she wanted to make sure Rascal, was out of harm's way here. She knew he had been neutered and gave me money to update his shots. It just didn't track with someone the dog didn't belong to," I said.

"How do you mean?" Captain Duffy asked.

"She wanted him to have all of his things, bed, toys, etc. Only someone who really cares about the dog and feels forced to give them up, worries about things like that," I said. "They want to send things that belong to the dog, like the bed or toys, thinking it will make the transition easier."

"It might be worth a follow up with her. I'll stop by her place tomorrow after we see where this sailboat is," Officer Bev said, and they left.

"It's three o'clock in the morning. If we're lucky, we can get five hours of sleep before they send over their tech wonder boy to see what you think those codes mean," Jiff said as we got in bed.

Jiff fell fast asleep and started snoring. The man could sleep anywhere. One Mardi Gras, we camped out early on the neutral ground all day to define our space for the Endymion Parade. Jiff fell asleep on our blanket while the parade passed and people stepped over him to get to their blankets. I had to wake him up when his friends' float approached so we could yell and get them to throw us stuff. I was still wired from the entire night and fell into a fitful sleep thinking about Abby and Ashley, wondering if what I thought was true. Something about the meeting on the pier kept coming back as odd. Was Ashley the one murdered and Abby convinced everyone it was really her so she could hide under her sister's identity? Jess seemed to think so, but Jess hadn't seen the woman who met us on the pier. Was it to escape her ex-husband or to escape with Big Al?

The next time I looked at the clock, it said four-thirty-two a.m. It was still dark outside, but it wouldn't be for long. I got up and went looking in the other bedrooms for something black to wear. I found a black pair of gym pants that were about three feet too long but I rolled the pants legs up to made them work. I found a long sleeve black T-shirt, also extremely large. I needed something to cover my head in black. In a drawer with some heavier clothes for cooler weather there was a black watchman cap… wool and hot.

When I put it on, I realized the eyes and mouth were cut out and it looked like a ski mask, the kind terrorists or bank robbers wear. Odd article of clothing for Florida, I thought. Maybe one of Jiff's brothers went snow skiing from Florida or maybe he just knocked off banks in his free time. Maybe he just left it here since it can get bitter cold on the beach on some winter days. I wondered how I'd bring this subject up to ask Jiff who it belonged to. I'd hate to have to tell Jiff how I found these clothes, rummaging around in his families' dressers, and then ask if any of them were bank robbers or terrorists. This was a mystery for another day.

After changing clothes, I logged into Jiff's computer and in less than a minute, I found out where Ashley Westlake lived, or the address of her home if she was the one who had been murdered. I wrote Jiff a note saying I was going to check out her address, but I'd call if I found anything and I'd be back before he woke up. Xoxo Brandy.

I really wanted to get back and return the covert wear before he woke up. At least, that was my plan. I took his car keys and drove to the address down the beach road. I found it quickly. It was only about a mile down the beach road away from Jiff's high rise. The GPS had me turn into a small subdivision on the other side of the highway fronting the bay. I could've walked. I drove slowly past her house.

Ashley had a private home, waterfront, on the bay which was really nice. There were windows all around the living area with views of the bay and some of the gulf. The home was raised so you could park under it or in the case of a storm, flood waters could pass through leaving the home intact. At least that was the thought in planning these raised residences.

There was something that looked like a lift under the middle area of the house. It was encased in wire mesh to allow any flood waters to pass through it as well. The front entrance had a grand stairway up to the front door on the second floor. It faced the street. I could see a stairway on the back of the home that lead to the beach and bay. I drove past and parked back on the road about a block away. I walked back to the house via the bay front so no one would see me on the street.

There was no one parked under her house so I climbed the back stairs to look through the windows. There was the old conch shell at the back door with the key in it. Really? Everyone at the beach used a conch shell as a hiding place, so why not try a flower pot or the fake rock? The bonus was Ashley had a plastic key ring on the key with codes which probably turned the security system on and off.

Oh boy, this was going to get interesting fast if I went in, activated the alarm, and these were not the codes to turn it off. Normally, I'm not a breaking and entering kinda gal but this was too much of a temptation. I tried the back door, and it was unlocked. I took a deep breath. I thought I'd say I saw it blown open and came up here to close it. Maybe Officer Bev would buy it. No way Duffy or Sorenson would.

I listened for a beeping sound that alerted you when the security system needed to be disarmed. The panel looked a lot like the one in my parents' home and it was near the door. The screen said ready to arm and there was no beeping. It had not been armed. I was good to go. If this was Abby and not Ashley living here, she, of all people, should use the security system. At the very least she should lock all the doors. It was becoming clear how she made a lot of her own problems.

The house was all on one level. The back stairs continued up to a flat roof to sunbath, watch a sunset or have cocktails. I didn't go up there.

I looked around inside. The door that was unlocked opened into a large den and kitchen adjoining. It had a cathedral ceiling which looked to be twenty feet or higher. Off the living area, I saw three large bedrooms. One was the master with a king size bed and one a guest room, also with a king size bed, and one was set up like an office. There was a bathroom between the office and guest room. The master was made up and undisturbed. I went into the master bath. It was clean with fresh towels on the towel bars. One towel was in the hamper. There was a makeup mirror on the vanity. All the makeup was carefully and well organized in the drawer. It was spotless. The closet in the room had nice clothes carefully hung by type, skirts all together, suits, jackets and so on. There was a floor to ceiling shoe rack with neatly paired shoes on it.

The guest room on the other hand was a wreck. The bed wasn't made, a suitcase sat opened on a luggage rack with clothes spilling out onto the floor all around it. Shoes looked like they had been kicked off and left anywhere from the front door to this bedroom. The hall bathroom that was a Jack and Jill type, accessible from both the guest room and the office. It was in shambles with towels on the floor. A travel make-up bag hung on the back of one door that opened into the office bedroom.

The vanity was cluttered with brushes and combs, haphazardly left where they were last used. Makeup powders dusted the vanity top. The closet held beautiful clothes on hangers in no particular order or grouping. There was a very nice white linen pants suit handing at one end. Had I not seen it recently, I would have known it had been worn by the wrinkles left in it.

The office where Ashley must have worked had a small computer desk with a MacBook open on it. A large square worktable stood in the middle of the room with a sewing machine at one end. It, too, was neat and tidy. I had snapped photos with my iPhone camera along the way.

It was clear to me who was who, and who came to the pier to meet us the other morning claiming to be Ashley. The thought struck me to take a hair brush from the master bedroom or bath and give it to Officer Bev. That was clearly Ashley's room and bath. It seemed Abby started out in the guest room and stayed there. I was looking for a hairbrush in the mess on the countertop in what I believed to be Abby's stuff in the guest room when I heard the front door open and voices. I ducked back into the office bedroom which was the furthest room from either front or back exit. I closed the door to the joint bathroom quietly.

It was a man and a woman's voice, and they were arguing.

"I can't believe you knew he ordered the hit on me," the woman said raising her voice.

"I didn't know. I never know what the money is paying for. He runs a tight ship, baby. I only tell one person where to drop the money. I had no idea it was for a hit on you," the man said. "Donnato always told me the money was for favors someone did for him. Abby, you have to believe me."

"How could you not put it together?" she said.

"You said he gave you no money in a settlement, so why would he want you dead?" the man asked. "Sounds to me like you were a gone pecan to him and he was moving on. Even if he knew you'd come here to be with your sister, you were out of his life. Why did he put a hit on you… unless… unless… did you take something of his and he wants it back?"

"No, I don't have anything of his. The dog was mine, only mine so it can't be that. Whoever he sent killed my sister by mistake and you had a part in it," the woman said. "All the times we talked about why he used your places down here for drops, you knew what he was doing."

Now I knew it was Abby Westlake, and I assumed the man's voice was Big Al. I hid in the closet in the guest bedroom with half sewn clothing pieces full of pins.

"I didn't know who it was supposed to be," the man said. "I only drop the money where he tells me. He sends the people to do the job, and he tells them where to pick up the money. He tells me where to put it. I tell Daniel."

"I know. I copied that list before I left. I had no idea I was on it," Abby said and started crying. "If I knew he planned to kill me, I would never have come here. I had no idea someone would mistake my sister for me. She didn't deserve this."

"Maybe he planned to kill your sister to scare you into returning whatever it is he thinks you have," Big Al said. "Oh, God, I hope he doesn't think you gave it to me. Who did you give that list to?"

"Ashley knew nothing about that. We went to some

lawyer here she used and gave each other our Power of Attorney. I had a second set of flash drives with that list on it and I gave it to that attorney to mail if anything happened to me. Donnato thought he was killing me, so maybe he'll stop looking for me now," she said.

"You didn't think this through. It's all over the paper that everyone thinks it's you who's dead. That attorney will mail those drives to whoever you told him to," Al said. "Your ex is gonna think you gave that list to me and I'm blackmailing him."

"Not if we leave."

"Look, we take the money from the drop before those two knuckleheads, Donnato sent down here, pick it up. I know where Daniel's dropping it later today. It's five-hundred large. That's a good bit and I have a ton of cash I can get my hands on. We'll get Daniel to take us to some island until all this blows over," Al said.

"This will never blow over if we take his five-hundred large. He'll figure out it was you, Al," she said.

"Okay, maybe we leave his money," he said.

"It will only be over when he's in prison for life which might involve him implicating you, Daniel and me," Abby said. "Did you think of that?"

"I'm gonna take a shower and think about this some more. You should think of moving into the master bedroom here in case anyone comes looking. That way you don't look like you're the guest," Al said.

"I'll do that if we stay. Right now, I think we ought to go on a vacation for a while. I've had a long day and just want to go to sleep," Abby said.

I heard the water running and the squeaky shower door open and close. I stepped into the hall so I could see Abby's reflection in the bedroom mirror. She was taking all her clothes off before she got into the bed. I heard the bed creaking as she made herself comfortable.

There was no better time to try to make my escape without being followed. I pulled the cap ski mask down over my face making sure my hair was hidden and I could see out of it. I took three deep breaths like I do in the gym before holding the really big breath to lift a weight or do the exercise. On the fourth breath, I jumped in front of her bedroom door and yelled so she saw what looked like a person breaking into her house. Abby started screaming and pulled the sheet over her head. I took off running out of the house down the front steps up the street to the car. I could still hear Abby screaming almost all the way to the car. There was no way she or Al was going to run up the street in a towel or call the police.

Chapter Sixteen

MY HEART WAS thumping like it was going to burst through the XXXL black T-shirt I still had on. It was five-thirty-eight a.m., when I got back to the condo and Jiff was still asleep. I put back the clothes and ski cap where I originally found them and went to make coffee. My heart was still racing and my hands still shaking by the time I got to the kitchen. I guess I'm a slow responder to a near miss or almost caught in the act.

I was well into my second cup of coffee studying the codes from the fifth flash drive when Jiff came into the kitchen. It was almost eight o'clock, and I felt like I had been at it all day. He had bed hair, and he was still groggy. I put a cup in front of him when he sat on a barstool at the island. He picked up the note I had left and read it.

"You didn't?" he asked.

"I did and I have the pictures to prove it," I said.

"Aren't you afraid someone will call the police on you for breaking and entering?"

"No, because the back door was open. No breaking,

just entering. Don't you want to know what I found out?"

"Since I will represent you if you are arrested, this is considered attorney/client privilege. Go on," he said with an over exaggerated exhale.

"Abby's things were in the guest room. Ashley's room is neat, bed's made, no sign of her using it or her office. Don't you think that's odd if the gal we met was really Ashley? Why isn't she staying in her own room? One used towel was in a hamper and the clean ones were on towel bars."

"I don't think anyone gets convicted based on clean or dirty towels or where you found them," Jiff said sipping his coffee. "Unless there's blood on them. Was there blood on them?"

"No, no blood. But... the guest room and guest bath were very much lived in with clothes, a man's and a woman's clothes, everywhere. That white linen suit we met the faux Ashley in on the pier was hanging in the guest closet, full of wrinkles."

"Failure to iron is a fashion felony, not a real one," he said taking a sip of his coffee.

"Here's the photos I took," I said and started to show him the photos on my cell.

"No, don't show me that. In fact, get rid of those. I never saw them," Jiff said a lot more awake now than he was a minute earlier.

It seemed to settle down when he thought I was deleting the photos.

"That's not all," I said.

"There's more?"

"Yes, I was there when Abby and Big Al came back. I hid in the third bedroom. Do you want to know what I heard?"

"You're gonna tell me anyway, right?"

"They were arguing. I heard Big Al call her Abby. She was angry with him for being involved with her sister's murder because she thought he knew what he was making the payoff for. They mentioned Daniel, the ex-husband in New York and Big Al suggested she move into Ashley's room in case anyone came snooping around."

"Did anyone see you?" Jiff asked.

"Well, sort of," I said. "That's really the part I shouldn't tell you."

"There's actually a part you don't want to tell me?" he said and looked up from his coffee. "I'm just glad you didn't get hurt, but I'm thrilled you didn't get caught."

I stood behind him and wrapped my arms around his neck. "I know when the money drop is with five-hundred large for Ashley's murder and I'm pretty sure it will be close to here. I need to talk to Bev."

We called Officer Bev who came over before the Cyber Crime tech arrived. The three of us sat in the condo kitchen at the island and I told Bev what I knew.

Jiff made it clear that he represented me. I was going to be a confidential informant as I came across information that was vital to the recent murder of the woman we found on the beach.

I told Bev everything I overheard Al and Abby saying at Ashley's house earlier. I said my curiosity got the better of me and I wanted to see if I could look through the windows and tell whether it was Abby or Ashley living there. That part was true. I never lied about what I actually did and she never asked for specifics. I said I was there snooping around when I heard them come home arguing. I failed to mention I was inside the house, hiding in a closet, when I heard them.

"I'll call my Captain and see if she found any sail plans filed with the Coast Guard on Daniel's boat or any of Al's boats. I don't think he does it, but we'll cover that base just in case," she said. "The Coast Guard should know where he is docked with that size boat and that might give us a good idea where the drop will take place."

"The time has been moved up from Wednesday to today. Wednesday was supposed to be the day Hot Rod overheard Al tell Daniel they had to change the day and place. I heard who I think was Al, tell someone who I think was Abby, that it was happening later today. This has got to be the same drop," I said.

Bev agreed. "It's more than what we've had to go on in the past."

"That's because information is relayed from one person to the next and no two people know more than one fact," I said.

"It leaves only one person knowing how to run the entire process," Jiff added. "But now Abby seems to know more, says she has copied incriminating files, and she is no longer restricted by marital privilege. This could be your chance to bust this syndicate unless she marries Big Al in the next few hours."

We all let out a groan. I hadn't even thought of that, and I didn't think the brain trust of Al and Abby had either.

Bev made a call to the FBI and the Coast Guard to update them. She asked the Coast Guard to find what port Daniel had *In Your Dreams* docked in currently. From the moment she hung up the day took off with everything happening faster than I would ever had imagined.

"This is how I think it works and after I see what the Cyber Crime guy comes up with, I might change my mind," I said. "Here's what I think…

"Abby's ex-husband in New York calls someone to do a job, or as Big Al referred to it, a favor. When the favor's done, NYC calls Al, says he needs money put at a location. Al could front the cash for NYC and get reimbursed from Daniel when he makes runs to the Caymans or B.V.I."

"That's how I think it works. Big Al gives Daniel the money to put in any one of a number of locations he owns, and the guys who did the favor pick it up," I explained.

"Daniel can get the money via boat, deliver the money the same way to any location Al has a drop point. He has boats in marinas from Slidell to Panama City and one or two in marinas on the east coast of Florida and in the Bahamas," Jiff said.

"Well, we're going to find out soon enough," Officer Bev said. "We'll have to keep eyes on Al and Daniel. Either one could make the drop."

Officer Bev got a call back a few minutes later and said Daniel's yacht, *In Your Dreams* was currently docked at a marina close to Panama City Beach. I looked through the files and the closest date to today was Wednesday and the drop was supposed to be at PCBM202. That was Panama City Beach Marina, Slip 202, and the number was 500L/MP. That should mean five-hundred thousand dollars to be picked up or paid to someone with initials MP.

I told Bev, she told the Coast Guard, the FBI and her Captain.

"I still think since the date changed, so did the drop location. If I were you, which I'm not, I'd put someone on Big Al and his slip in the Destin Beach Marina watching his fishing boat and this one in Panama City Beach," I said. "Just a suggestion."

Bev called it in to her Captain who sent a detective to sit on Big Al's Fishing Boat and follow him if he goes out to it. I mentioned he might be staying at Ashley Westlake's home right up the highway. Bev just looked at me and relayed Big Al's possible whereabouts to her Captain.

"Uh huh, got it. Okay," Bev said and hung up. "Gotta go, but you two stay put, as in, stay here, go to the pool or the beach but stay close to your phones. I'll call you when we have something."

The tech from Cyber Crime was arriving as Bev was leaving. I told him I thought we had it all resolved but if we didn't I'd get in touch with him through Officer Bev.

Jiff and I headed to the pool. Nothing like a cool dip to clear your head of cobwebs from a night with little to no sleep.

🐕 🐕 🐕 🐕 🐕 🐕 🐕 🐕 🐕 🐕

MUCH LATER THAT day, after a nap, we went lounging in the pool on rafts working on our sunburns. We were having a very late lunch poolside when Officer Bev and Captain Duffy came looking for us. As much as I tried to avoid Wallace, he seemed to run into us every time we left the condo. I wasn't sure he ever made the connection it was me at the All Male Review. He showed Bev and Duffy out to where we were eating.

"You two are quite the pair," Captain Duffy said. "I don't know how you put it together, but your willingness to stick around and offer your help while on vacation cracked this wide open. You want to tell us how you figured out what they were doing?"

"Rascal was the linchpin. I can only tell you what I saw after we found the flash drives," I said. "I saw an entry DHM108. The night we went to Big Al's World Famous Tiki Hut, we strolled along the piers and I saw that number on Big Al's slip for his Fishing Boat in the Destin Harbor Marina. As soon as I saw it I thought, I know what all the codes mean now. I just didn't know how they connected until I saw Daniel with Big Al at the All Male Review and Rod told me Al was meeting with the guy who moves his money."

"You won't guess who we caught at Big Al's dock box picking up the drop?" Officer Bev said. "The initials MP belonged to…"

"Mike Perricone," I said. "I wish I could say I'm surprised. I wish I had figured it would be him but it just came to me when you said his initials. I thought it would be one of those two guys who roughed up Daniel and who may have killed Ashley Westlake."

"They worked for Perricone. Mike became disenchanted with law enforcement when the FBI booted him over to us so he went to the dark side," Captain Duffy explained. "Mike made the arrangements, picked up the money drops, taking his cut for the crimes the other two did."

"We've picked them all up, Abby, Al, Mike and Daniel. Seems they all want a deal except Daniel. He claims he was just a courier. I'm so disappointed in Perricone," Bev said. "After he showed us those drives you gave him, I always had the feeling he was holding out, that maybe he doctored those drives before we saw them. I need to go back to see if his initials are on any of those entries."

"We have a copy of what we gave him, if you want it," Jiff said. "We opened them to see what they were, and I saved a copy for evidence in case it was ever needed."

Captain Duffy handed Jiff her card and asked him to email all the files he had to her.

"We should have made the connection that Perricone was involved since he knew Daniel, knew Al, but we didn't know if he knew Ashley and Abby," Jiff said.

"He knew them," Officer Bev said.

"Doesn't matter. You gave us the time and place. We caught him red handed, on video. Mike Perricone picked up the money from Big Al's dock box in the Panama City Marina around eleven this morning," Captain Duffy said. "Before we could mirandize him he was asking for a deal."

"What's gonna happen to Daniel?" Jiff asked.

"That's for the courts to decide but he is cooperating," Area Director Steve Sorenson walked up to us adding. "He's trying to say he had no part in anything illegal since he was only a courier and didn't know what he was moving. He might do time on tax evasion or money laundering unless he can give us more on the big fish in NYC. That's the very least the FBI will charge him on."

"I'll never forgive him for almost giving Rascal to those two thugs who showed up that night. It looked like he was going to until Jiff yelled at them, and those guys took off," I said.

"Actually," Officer Bev said, "I asked him about that. Daniel maintained he does not know those two, but he saw Perricone that morning at the West Marine boat supply store right after he picked up Rascal. Perricone didn't mention the murder but asked him if he got a dog. Daniel said he found him. Perricone knew who the dog belonged to and never bothered contacting you. I'm sure he sent those men to the pier and to your condo."

"He called Donnato Neglio and told him where Abby's dog was," Captain Duffy said and looked at Sorenson.

He continued, "Donnato figured he could use the dog as leverage but never got the chance. Some rookie gave Abby the info on where the dog was and everything was signed off and dog removed to New Orleans before Mike could give Donnato an update. Since we thought it was Ashley acting on Abby's behalf, we told Perricone and he relayed the wrong info back to NYC. He told them they fulfilled the contract on Abby Westlake, Donnato's ex-wife. Matter closed. Money owed."

"No one knew about the new flash drive yet, least of all Neglio, Perricone and Big Al. I think that kept Abby alive," Officer Bev added.

"Well, I feel better knowing Daniel is absolved of trying to hurt the dog, but he knew what he was doing. He knew it was in no way legit," Jiff added. "Business—real business moves money via bank transfers and wires. Who moves cash around on cigarette boats in waterproof duffle bags and makes deposits in lock boxes or gym lockers? This guy went to law school and he should be held accountable at a higher standard."

"He'll be answering questions for a while on money laundering," Sorenson said. He thanked us and made his goodbyes.

"What's going to happen with Abby and Big Al?" I asked Bev and Duffy. "You know if Abby never made copies of those flash drives, this would have kept going until one of them made a mistake and you may never have caught them. She's the reason all this came to an end."

"According to Jess, Abby came to visit at least once sometimes twice a month. She always went to Big Al's... for the music," Officer Bev said. "On occasion she would drag Ashley along who stayed for one drink with her sister and then left because Big Al would start hanging around Abby. Jess says it was because Abby was still in love with Al and he was still in love with her."

Captain Duffy let out an uh, uh, uh of disapproval over the Abby, NYC, Big Al love triangle. "She told us during her interrogation that she and Al planned to disappear together. When Donnato wanted a divorce, she saw it as a way out for her, but not for Al. She made copies of the flash drives thinking they could use them to get him out. Or at the very least, get them mailed to the FBI to give Donnato more to worry about than finding her. They received a copy today from the attorney those two went to see last week since everyone, including me, thought Abby was the one murdered."

"Abby said Donnato didn't know about her and Al. Donnato liked his operation running smoothly and Al did that for him. He'd kill her before he'd kill Al," Officer Bev added.

"When are you two leaving? I'm sorry if this took over your entire vacation here," Captain Duffy said.

Jiff and I looked at each other. "We called back home and are staying another two days. We'll be leaving Thursday."

"Really? I have another case I'd like to run by you to see…" Captain Duffy tried to say before Jiff cut her off.

"No, no, no," Jiff said pulling me into the pool.

"How do you know we won't want to help?" I asked him.

"I want at least two days' vacation with you before we help solve anymore crimes!"

The End

About the Author

Colleen Mooney was born and raised in New Orleans along with everyone else in her family. She is a Wall Street Journal Best Selling Author and writes a cozy mystery series set in New Orleans called *The New Orleans Go Cup Chronicles* and the fifth book, *Dog Gone and Dead* is released in July 2018 in the boxed set Summer Snoops and Cozy Crimes: 12 Cozy Mysteries for the Dog Days of Summer. She and the eleven other authors are donating all proceeds from the sale of this boxed set to two no kill animal shelters.

In January 2017 Colleen organized a Sisters in Crime chapter in New Orleans, has been elected President and has a planned a Mystery Writers' Conference for June. She is currently working on her 6th book in the Brandy Alexander series, *Politicians, Potholes and Pralines!*

Colleen worked in corporate America for twenty-one years before retiring and has lived in Birmingham, Atlanta, New Jersey and New York. She moved back to New Orleans every time before another corporate reorganization would transfer her to another city. She says, "New Orleanians are a lot like boomerangs or homing pigeons. The minute we move away, we start trying to move back."

In New Orleans, she's been a member and active in many Mardi Gras Krewes, Super Krewes, and organizations. Colleen says she has never met a parade she didn't like.

She's an ardent animal lover and the Director for a breed rescue, Schnauzer Rescue of Louisiana for the last fifteen years. She has rescued and placed over 350 abandoned or surrendered Schnauzers. Find her rescue on Facebook facebook.com/NOLASchnauzerRescue or the rescue Website www.nolaschnauzer.com. She loves to write, and writes about what she loves. Colleen says, "New Orleans is where it all happens for me."

Keep in touch with Colleen here:

My website:

www.colleenmooney.com

Amazon Colleen Mooney books:

amazon.com/Colleen-Mooney/e/B00N9I5DMK

Facebook:

facebook.com/colleen.mooney.716

Twitter:

twitter.com/mooney_colleen

Goodreads Author Profile:

goodreads.com/author/show/8548635.Colleen_Mooney

BookBub:

bookbub.com/profile/colleen-mooney

www.ingramcontent.com/pod-product-compliance
Lightning Source LLC
Chambersburg PA
CBHW070955120726
47910CB00004B/1243